Wáchale!

Poetry and Prose About Growing Up Latino in America

edited by Ilan Stavans

Cricket Books
A Marcato Book
Chicago

Printed in the United States of America

Designed by Anthony Jacobson

First edition, 2001

Library of Congress Cataloging-in-Publication Data

Wachale! : poetry and prose on growing up Latino in America / edited by
Ilan Stavans.—1st ed.

    p. cm.

Includes bibliographical references.

Summary: A bilingual collection of poems, stories, and other writings
that celebrates diversity among Latinos.

   ISBN 0-8126-4750-5 (cloth : alk. paper)

   1. Children's literature, American—Hispanic American authors. 2.
Children's literature, Latin American. 3. Hispanic Americans—Literary
collections. 4. Hispanic Americans—Juvenile literature. [1. Hispanic
Americans—Literary collections. 2. American literature—Hispanic
American authors—Collections. 3. Spanish language
materials—Bilingual.] I. Stavans, Ilan.

   PZ5 .W12 2001

   810.8'09282'08968--dc21

   [Fic]

                                                2001047189

Para Ana Gladis Sánchez,
refugee
from El Salvador

CONTENTS

Contents

III. P'ATRÁS Y P'ALANTE

IV. SPEAKIN' LA VOZ

Contents

WÁCHALE!

Un gringo I knew in my mexicano days used to say to me: Ilancho mi güero, cada persona is born with a limited amount of cuentos. What a lástima if they are never let out!

Este sampler of almost treinta cuentos y canciones, told by gente like you and yo, are from and about nuestras raíces—our *rootas.*

You'll be surprised by what these cuenteros have to say: Hablan de amor y de growing up, de alegría and of hope too.

They are boricuas, chicanos, cubanitos, y demás, all from los Unaited Steits, with ancestros from across la border, del mundo hispanic. Sus carácteres buy grocerías, juegan beis, and remembrean their historia—that is, they janguean day-in day-out.

Más que nada, what you'll find in this libro is a new lengua, mixteada, with a lot of feelin.

Lucky estos cuentos have been let out, don't you think? They are no longer prisioneros of their tellers. Ya no son de sus dueños but ours, yours and míos.

De verdá that what I most like in them is . . . pues, the sense of hogar they evoke together: Home, sweet home. Our jefes y jefas are often inmigrantes: they've built a vida un poco en español and a bit in English. Home is never pure, o sí? Ni tampoco perfect. And it generates todo tipo de feelins.

Pero al final el hogar is where we feel most cómodos, isn't it right? Como reyes y reinas in our private hud. Qué más can one ask?

Wáchale, broder! These voices are from el corazón.

Introduction

Wáchale (WA-tcha-leh), *interj.: Spanglish for look out, be aware, watch out. The action of watching or looking out for something. Mark Twain,* Huck Finn: *"I never tried to do anything, but just poked along low-spirited and on the watchout." Guillermo Gómez Peña,* Codex Spanglishicus: *"Wáchale, carnal! Let's speak for ourselves . . . "*

As we begin a new century and a new millennium, America isn't getting older but younger . . . and astonishingly diverse, too. Hispanics are already its largest minority, some 40 million strong. (The U.S. Census Bureau actually puts the number at 35 million, but that includes only citizens and legal residents, and not undocumented people.) Our youthful presence is felt everywhere, from music to politics, from baseball to literature. That youthfulness is a challenge, though. The average age for Latinos is between thirteen and twenty-five, which is significantly younger than other groups. And the average family income is lower than that of other segments of society. Though the numbers make it clear that we are here, Americans in general still have very little sense of who we Latinos are, where we come from, and what our dreams and aspirations are.

This anthology is a sampler of what is already in store and a promise of things to come, selected with an eye to reaching readers who are in their own transitions from childhood into their teens. The experience of growing up Latino north of the Río Grande is, first and foremost, about the clash of cultures. Those of us described as Hispanic—the term to some is appropriate, while to others it is offensive—trace their roots in a larger geography of republics that range from Mexico in the north to Chile and Argentina in the south, from Colombia to the Dominican Republic. These republics have been more or less racially mixed from the start. Thus, the immigrants who have settled in the United States from the mid-nineteenth century to the present are *mestizos,* whites, Africans, and Asians. Almost all of them are unified by a common language, Spanish, although Brazil, the Guianas, and portions of the Caribbean Basin speak Portuguese patois, French, or English. Some of us arrived here wealthy, others with nothing at all. Immigrants to *El Norte,* be they from Havana, Managua, or Bogotá, have come from the lower, middle, and upper strata in Latin America.

In attempting to build a mosaic, I have selected memoirs, poems, and stories from different national groups, different backgrounds, and, of equal importance, different generations. For Hispanics, as a community, are not, by any stretch of the imagination, a new feature in the American landscape. Their ancestry dates back to colonial times, when Spanish missionaries and *exploradores* settled in Florida and the Southwest. While we speak about the new Hispanic presence in America, we could just as accurately talk about the Latinos who were here long before the English arrived. The sense of tradition, of rootedness, comes through, for instance, in Jovita González's reformulations of border folk tales and in Cecilio García-Camarillo's poem "Talking to the Río Grande," to give a couple of examples. Just the opposite mood comes through in other pieces, such as Rosaura Sánchez's "jac$in$the$bag," which capture the shock of the new, the feeling that for Hispanics life in English began just yesterday.

My overall title is a favorite street expression. It announces the freshness that results from the old and the new, as does my short call-to-arms "Wáchale!," which precedes this introduction. For Spanglish, a hybrid, is a way of communicating that arises out of life as we live it now. Every day on the street, via the radio, in signs, songs, e-mails, slogans, advertisements, news headlines, and jokes, we hear, read, and speak English and Spanish, and make both our own. This is our duty, for full mastery of both languages is a necessity in order for us to succeed. Still, this explains why I have included, in generous fashion, material that is, either fully or partially, but always unapologetically, in Spanglish. In my opinion, it is the hybrid that is us, now.

Literature is a game of mirrors: in it we see our faces reflected a thousand times, in different shapes and forms. It wasn't easy for me to choose the selections for this volume. Numerous academic ethnographic and historical books are available about Latino experiences, and the number of first-hand accounts drafted with an adult audience in mind has mushroomed in the last couple of decades. But literature for younger readers still is, unforgivably, minimal. Is this because Latinos don't produce it? The answer is no, with an exclamation point. Just the opposite: there is a copious library waiting for readers to browse its shelves. So why did I have difficulty collecting material for my young readers?

Most of what is available is targeted toward a mature public. It is about assimilation, about the act—and art—of appreciating the present by reinventing the past. Few authors use the voice I had in mind, one that isn't condescending, and that explores growing up with an open heart and a vivid style. Only a handful of Latino authors have committed themselves to children's literature, and a majority of them aim young, for picture book readers. For too many other authors, Hispanics are still seen as "exotic," as not yet fully American. Not enough of us yet see writing for middle schoolers and teenagers as what we want to do, and too few publishers have committed themselves to finding authors and artists to write those books.

This approach ought to change immediately. It is in the hands of editors, teachers, and parents to encourage such a change. The prevailing approach is based on a false preconception that young Latinos do not want to read about themselves, or that non-Latino adults will not be curious to learn more about their classmates and neighbors. My own conversations with countless adolescents of Hispanic background reveal a far different reality: a passion to read is tangible, but adolescent readers have a terrible time finding books that speak about their own odyssey. This results in alienation: the material they come across is only about sports (Roberto Clemente has become the stand-in for everything Latino boys can feel proud of), about pop stars, or about harsh life in the fields or in gangs. What about the ups and downs of everyone else?

A few years into the future I want to come back to this anthology and do it again—with, I trust, a generous amount of freshly made material to add. The readers of *Wáchale!* will be its authors.

Editor's Note

A number of poems and one story appear here in translation. The English version always comes first, followed by the Spanish. The translator's name precedes the translation.

I

RÁPIDO,
RÁPIDO

JACSINSTHESBAG

Rosaura Sánchez   **Translated by Beatrice Pita**

"Dice it, chop it, peel it . . ." Rosaura Sánchez uses fiction to reflect on the life of south-of-the-border immigrants to the United States. She is a professor at the University of California in San Diego. The following story, originally in Spanish and included in He Walked In and Sat Down, and Other Stories, *is about nameless workers paid to prepare burritos, a Tex-Mex dish, without ever being allowed to have input in the process. Is the burrito an authentic Mexican dish when recently arrived Mexicans don't have the slightest idea what it is and how it is prepared?*

> Chop it up, chop it up, dice it, dice it.
> Trim the ends, peel the onion,
> Chop it up, chop it up, dice it, dice it.
> Chop, chop, chop.
> Dice, dice, dice.
> Slide it off, slide it off, into the pan.
> Chop, chop, chop.
> Dice, dice, dice, slide it off,
> get it right.
> Into the pan.
> Trim the ends,
> peel it.
> Chop, chop, chop,
> dice, dice, dice.
> Faster, faster.
> Chop, chop.
> Dice, dice.
> Into the pan.

Dump it in, dump it in.
Chop, peel, chop, dice.
Chop, peel, chop, dice.
Peel them first, three at a time.
Chop off the ends.
Chop, chop, chop.
Dice, dice, dice.
Corti, corti, corti, y zas!
Slide it off.
Faster, faster.
Chop, dice, pan,
chop, dice, pan.
Híjole, careful with the knife.
Chop, chop,
turn the onion.
Keep your eye on the knife,
Jeez . . . I can't see.
My eyes, my eyes, my nose.
Sniff, sniff, sniff.
Man, *ya no aguanto.*
I can't see, I can't see anymore.
What a stink! The tears,
the onions.
Qué peste!
Chop, chop, chop,
dice, dice, dice.
Don't drop them, now,
slide, slide, slide them into the pan.
Dale, dale.
Chop, chop,
dice, dice,
into the pan.
Onions, onions, onions
nothing but more onions,

cuánta cebolla,
onions diced for *tacos,*
onions for *enchiladas*
onions, onions, onions,
corti, corti, corti,
chop, chop, chop,
dice, dice, dice.
slide it off, slide it off.
I can't stand it, I can't stand it anymore.
Man, my eyes, my eyes.
Peel, chop, dice,
slide it off, slide it off . . .

"O.K., Mere. *Ya párale.* You can go on break for lunch."

"Hey, Viken, I tell you I just can't stand it. The smell, really, it's too much. I'm getting this splitting headache, *'mana.*"

"*Mira,* I think they're gonna transfer you over to the tortilla section, anyway, 'cause you're way too slow, *vas muy despacio y ya anda repelando el mayordomo.* You know, the manager, he's already griping about your going too slow."

Thirty minutes later.

"*Oye,* Viken, you better show me what I have to do here."

"O.K., look, Mere, the tortillas drop from this belt and all you have to do is fill them and then just roll them. See, like this. You take the tortilla, stuff it with the meat and onion filling over here in this huge pan, and then roll it. You place the *burritos* on these long trays that they pick up every fifteen minutes to take them where they get wrapped in foil. Got it? But you have to stay on top of it and move fast, 'cause the tortillas just keep coming. Just don't let them pile up like this 'cause you'll be in big trouble with the line manager. O.K., that's it, that's the way, that's the way. You got it. Careful, there, Mere, or you'll get burned. Pick them up with your fingertips. *Ándale,*

ándale, así nomás. All right, all right. I'll see you later. I have to go back to my station. Today they've got me doing wrapping."

> *Ay!* They're hot.
> Flatten it, stuff it, roll it.
> Flatten it, stuff it, roll it.
> Flatten it, stuff it, roll it.
> *Dobla y dobla y dobli, dobli, dobli.*
> Jeez! I'm getting burned.
> Man, they're coming out super hot!
> Come on. Gotta keep up.
> Fold it, stuff it, fill it, roll it.
> Stuff, stuff, stuff,
> roll, roll, roll.
> *Híjole,* these tortillas just keep coming in, just keep coming.
> Stuff, roll, stuff, roll, stuff, roll. *Doblidoblidobli,*
> ¡*Ay! mequemoimequemoimequemo.*
> Too hot!
> Oww!
> My fingers!
> Stuff it, fold it, no, roll it,
> *Ay!* What was it?
> It's not a *taco,* it's a *burrito.*
> I'm getting all mixed up.
> Roll it, roll it.
> Flatten it out,
> stuff it, roll it.
> Stuff it, roll it,
> stuff and roll.

Oh, no! Here comes the boss.

"Hey, honey, you're doing O.K. for a starter. See if you can go a little faster tomorrow, though."

Kennedy in the Barrio

Judith Ortiz Cofer

Judith Ortiz Cofer was born in Hormigueros, Puerto Rico, in 1952. She teaches at the University of Georgia, Athens. She is the author of several books for young adults, including The Year of Our Revolution: New and Selected Poems and Stories, *in which she explores the life of a teenager known as María Elena and also as Mary Ellen, her Latina and Anglo selves.*

My sixth-grade class had been assigned to watch the Kennedy inauguration on television, and I did, at the counter of Puerto Habana, the restaurant where my father worked. I heard the Cuban owner Larry Reyes say that an Irish Catholic being elected meant that someday an *hispano* could be president of the United States, too. I saw my father nod in automatic agreement with his boss, but his eyes were not on the grainy screen; he was concerned with the food cooking in the back and with the listless waitress mopping the floor. Larry Reyes turned his attention to me and then raised his cup as if to make a toast: "Here's to a *puertorriqueño* or *puertorriqueña* president of the United States," he laughed, not kindly, I thought. "Right, Elenita?"

I shrugged my shoulders. Later my father would once again reprimand me for not showing Mr. Reyes the proper amount of respect.

Two years and ten months later, I would run to Puerto Habana on a cold Friday afternoon to find a crowd gathered around a television set. Many of them, men and women alike, were sobbing like children. *"Dios mío, Dios mío,"* they kept wailing. A group of huddling women tried to embrace me as I made my way to my parents, who were holding each other tightly, apart from the others. I slipped in between them. I smelled her scent of castile soap, *café con leche,* and cinnamon; I inhaled his mixture of sweat and Old Spice cologne, a man-smell that I was afraid to like too much.

That night at Puerto Habana Larry Reyes and my father served free food. Both of them wore black armbands. My mother cooked and I bused tables. An old woman started reciting the rosary aloud, and soon practically everyone was kneeling on that hard linoleum floor, praying and sobbing for our dead president. Exhausted from the outpouring of public grief and exasperated by the displays of uncontrolled emotion I had witnessed that day, the *ay benditos,* the kisses and embraces of strangers I had had to endure, I asked if I could go home early. For the first time, my vigilant mother trusted me to walk alone at night without the usual lecture about the dangers of the streets. The dark, empty silence of our apartment gave me no solace, and in a turmoil of emotions I had never experienced before, I went to sleep the night of the day President Kennedy died. I rose the next day to a world that looked the same.

MY CUBAN BODY

Carolina Hospital

Carolina Hospital is a Cuban American poet, translator, and writer. Under the pseudonym C. C. Medina, she cowrote with her husband the novel A Little Love. *This recollection is about growing up as a Cuban teenage girl among Anglo classmates, and about making peace with one's own qualities.*

"Hot pants" is what we called the very tight shorts we used to wear in the '70s. One hot Friday night when I was fifteen years old, I sneaked out of the house wearing a shiny blue plastic raincoat over my hot pants and my spandex tube top. It was Mami's idea to put on the raincoat over the hot pants. She wanted to avoid Papi's anger when he saw my clothes, or lack of them. My petite older sister (by two years), two inches shorter and thirty pounds lighter, dressed the same way. So what was the problem? The problem was that I was younger but I had developed sooner. Plus, the fashion in the '70s only helped to attract attention to my early development. It was impossible to hide curves and protrusions within minuscule pieces of cloth or skintight polyester blouses and pants. In Papi's eyes, I was flaunting my womanhood, yet I didn't have the maturity to deal with its consequences. His instincts were right, but his volatile approach was not.

That night I eagerly went to my classmate's party. My sister and I walked into the screened patio in the back of the house where the stereo had been set up. I removed the raincoat. Immediately, all eyes were on me. I felt self-conscious, yet as I danced slowly with different boys—for us, success was measured in slow dance—I discovered the power of the flesh.

I felt exhilarated by my ability to attract the opposite sex. However, I also felt the fear of unleashing a power I had little control over. In addition, my father's anger and my mother's collusion sent me mixed messages. Was there something wrong with my emerging womanhood? Instead of enjoying my new curves, I began to feel shame and embarassment.

I also had to deal with the fact that I was different from most of my petite blond classmates. Being rounder, shorter, and hairier than they was a great source of anguish. My solution was to diet, straighten my hair, and wear platform shoes, the highest I could tolerate. But the damage was done. I grew up unhappy with my physical appearance, always self-conscious of my looks.

Mother didn't help. It wasn't that she disliked my looks. The opposite: she constantly noticed and complimented the very things I wanted to forget. For instance, she always told me I was lucky to have thighs and calves which were beautifully endowed, not thin and scrawny like hers. She believed I had inherited their thickness from my father's Catalán side. That was the last thing I wanted to hear, that I looked like my short, overweight, bear-like hairy father (by Anglo standards) with whom I did not get along during my teen years.

Ironically, my mother also suffered growing up because of her physical appearance. She was often called a tomboy and was fed thick mango and papaya shakes in the hopes that she would put more fat on her bones. You see, for the Havana of the 1930s and '40s, she was too thin and too tall at five feet seven. Plus she lacked the thick, long, wavy hair I so detested in myself. That is why as she watched me diet, exercise, and straighten my hair, day in and day out, she would say, perplexed, how growing up, she would have given anything to have had the physical traits I so rejected in myself. I didn't understand or care. I wasn't living in Havana. I was living in the land of Twiggy.

Back then no one talked about being anorexic, but that is exactly what Twiggy looked like—a beautiful anorexic gazelle with long, blond, perfectly straight hair that probably weighed more than she did. Soon all the models became Twiggy look-alikes, and she became the standard for us to aim for, an impossible goal for a Cubanita with already emerging curves and protrusions—but what did I know?

I wish I had known that beauty comes in all sizes and shapes and that the media promotes artificial standards of beauty. It would have helped me to understand that people's perceptions of beauty are shaped by the culture and the times they belong to. For instance, what was undesirable in the Havana of my mother's youth was longed for in mine. I have tried to explain these things to my own daughter, now a teenager.

Just the other day, she pointed out to me how Marilyn Monroe weighed 160 pounds when she was America's most admired sex symbol. Of course, that was before the age of Twiggy. But perhaps her awareness, especially growing up in a city like Miami full of cultural diversity, will help her and her peers become more tolerant of themselves and their appearances. Perhaps being different will be easier for them than it was for me.

One rainy afternoon, I sat in the back of Sister Helen's class, sleepily listening to her read classic love poems. I soon grew tired of hearing about angelic ladies with alabaster skin, hazel eyes, and golden hair. Suddenly, a sonnet by Shakespeare shook me from my stupor.

My Mistress' Eyes Are Nothing Like the Sun

My mistress' eyes are nothing like the sun;
Coral is far more red than her lips' red;
If snow be white, why then her breasts are dun;

If hair be wires, black wires grow on her head.
I have seen roses damasked, red and white,
But no such roses see I in her cheeks,
And in some perfumes is there more delight
Than in the breath that from my mistress reeks.
I love to hear her speak, yet well I know
That music hath a far more pleasing sound.
I grant I never saw a goddess go;
My mistress when she walks treads on the ground.
And yet, by heaven, I think my love as rare
As any she belied with false compare.

That afternoon, Shakespeare's verses filled me with hope. I felt redeemed. Perhaps out there existed a young Shakespeare who would find beauty in my own brown wires and raspy voice, who didn't mind my heavy treads and olive flesh. Shakespeare's words taught me an unforgettable lesson about the force of words while validating my own reality. That sonnet planted a seed. Yet, it took many more years, marriage, and motherhood for me to finally be pleased with my Cuban body. It shouldn't have to take that long.

Talking to the Río Grande

Cecilio García-Camarillo

Cecilio García-Camarillo was born in 1943. He is a poet, journalist, radio newscaster, and an important voice in the Chicano movement. (Beginning in the 1960s, this was both a political and an artistic effort to recognize and honor Mexican Americans in the United States.) His work is vivid and gives voice to the oral tradition in which Spanish and English interact.

Siempre regreso a ti, my source, you gnarled piece of liquid leather. When I feel good or reventado you're always there for me. Solamente your indifference tiene la capacidad de entender the outpourings of my soul. As a child in Loredo I knew you as the powerful divider of a people who were once one and the same, y ahora de aquel lado están los mexicanos, y acá, nosotros, los tejanos. You flowed on doing your own thing, not caring about the weird games men play. I swam in you and your dark waters mixed with my blood. Toda mi vida he permanecido cerca de ti 'cause I have the need to reveal myself to you so that I can cope con todas las chingaderas de la vida. Listen to me old one, and help make her love me once again . . .

  ¿Pero cómo jodidos le hago para resolver la situación? Old river, how can I reject with my body la maña of wanting to own her? ¿Cómo puedo dejar de ser lo que soy? How? I'd have to die and be reborn. If I were a rattlesnake and could change skins, I'd be renewed. I'd be young with a glistening new skin. I'd drink your waters with a new soul. Maybe then I wouldn't have the need of wanting her by my side. I'd even be able to forgive my father. To be renewed, but first I'd have to die.

I almost died once, remember? Yes, I was in junior high, and my friends from school and I played hooky, and I took them in my old car to the family ranch. Man, aquellos sí eran tiempos locotes. And then I showed them something special, la noria, so deep and mysterious. I remember my cousins Kiko and Pepe digging it years before, and I was always afraid to get close to it. But now my friends were right up to the rim of the well, and they saw some snakes at the bottom. They got all excited and started shooting at them with .22-caliber rifles. I yelled no, son víboras negras, they're harmless. Estan alla abajo porque hay ratas y se las van a comer. But they just kept shooting like maniacs. Then they argued about who was going to go down the ladder to get the snakes so we could take them back to Laredo and scare the shit out of people, but nobody had the guts to volunteer. Then someone said I should do down 'cause after all it was my ranch and I was used to those kinds of things, and they circled me and called me joto, miedoso, chicken shit, and pussy. My heart started jumping all over the place, but I decided to go down anyway. I'd show them que mi verga estaba más gruesa than all of theirs put together.

I started going down and it felt warm, with a tightness and then a release, as if the dark and damp well were pulsating. There was a thick old smell all around. I could barely see the bottom, but I knew the snakes were dead, probably killed twenty times over. I went lower, trying to focus on the snakes. The well now felt cool and exhilarating. Suddenly, I saw movement all around me. I couldn't believe that the dark walls were moving all around me. Then I realized there were thousands of crickets living there and the shooting had agitated them. I stood still and looked at them for a moment. They were like a black blanket moving in waves. Then my friends again me rayaron la madre and even threw stones, and I felt so alone and scared. The crickets got even more excited when my foot slipped and I almost fell. With one hand I braced myself against the wall of the well, but when I did that the crickets began jumping. I felt their cool and spiny legs all over my body, and then they started chirping, first a few chirping soft-ly, then more. I had my balance now, then by the thousands the crickets were chirping louder and louder all around me. Their song relaxed me, and I did not feel scared of them any-more. It seemed as if they were playing their cricket song so that I wouldn't hear my drunk father or my friends yelling obscenities. I didn't care about falling off the ladder or about the snakes. The rhythm of the crickets' song kept coming into me, filling up my mind and every part of my body like a soothing dream. I knew my face was smiling, yes, I was at peace with myself for the first time in my life, and at that moment that is all that mattered in the world. The song of the crickets and I became one.

Mexicans Begin Jogging

Gary Soto

Award-winning Chicano poet, author, and editor Gary Soto was born in Fresno, California, in 1952. His favorite audience is children and young adults, and he has written many lively books for them, such as Canto Familiar *and* Junior College. *His characters are Mexican in Anglo neighborhoods. This melodious poem, like the song "Deportee," is about the maltreatment of Mexican illegal workers in the United States.*

At the factory I worked
In the fleck of rubber, under the press
Of an oven yellow with flame,
Until the border patrol opened
Their vans and my boss waved for us to run.
"Over the fence, Soto," he shouted,
And I shouted that I was American.
"No time for lies," he said, and pressed
A dollar in my palm, hurrying me
Through the back door.

Since I was on his time, I ran
And became the wag to a short tail of Mexicans—
Ran past the amazed crowds that lined
The street and blurred like photographs, in rain.
I ran from that industrial road to the soft
Houses where people turned at the turn of an autumn sky.
What could I do but yell *vivas*
To baseball, milkshakes, and those sociologists

Who would clock me
As I jog into the next century
On the power of a great, silly grin.

CORRAN, MEXICANOS, CORRAN
Translated by Ilan Stavans

Trabajo en la factoría
Con la goma moteada, bajo la presión
De un amarillo horno en llamas.
Hasta que llega la migra
Sus camiones y mi jefe anunciando nuestra huída.
"Sáltate la reja, Soto," me gritó,
Y yo le grité de vuelta que soy americano.
"Déjate de bromas," replicó, empujando
un dólar contra la palma de mi mano, apresurándome
rumbo a la puerta de atrás.

Estaba a su disposición, así que corrí
Y pasé a ser la punta de una cola de mexicanos—
Corrí frente a la asombrada masa de mirones
Enfilados en la calle y borrosos como fotografías en la
    lluvia.
Corrí de esa avenida industrial hasta las suaves
Casas donde la gente se arrejunta bajo un sol otoñal.
Qué podía hacer sino gritar Qué viva . . .
El béisbol, las malteadas, y eso sociólogos
Que se divierten estudiándome,
Mientras corro rumbo al próximo milenio,
Con el poder de una amplia y juguetona sonrisa.

LA LLORONA

Alcina Lubitch Domecq   **Translated by Ilan Stavans**

Alcina Lubitch Domecq, born in Guatemala in 1953, lives in Jerusalem. Her father was sent to Auschwitz by the Nazis because he was Jewish. He survived, but the terrible experience in the concentration camp left a deep mark of depression on him. In her work Lubitch Domecq tries to understand the experience her father went through, and the life he led as an immigrant to Guatemala City. The following story is a variation on the Mexican folk tale of the Weeping Woman, who is forced to abandon her children. In this haunting rendition La Llorona becomes an immigrant.

This rendition of the mythic tail of La Llorona takes place in Ciudad Juaréz.

She was, as everyone knows, a betrayed woman. After her husband left her without a single centavo, La Llorona and her three children tried to cross the border to the United States. She sold all her belongings in the town not far from Chetumal, the capital of Quintana Roo, where poverty reigns. A distant relative in Arizona (a nephew of her stepfather), to whom she had sent a desperate word, replied several months later saying he wasn't wealthy enough to provide her with the tickets but if she moved to *el otro lado,* the other side, he knew of a *niñera* always helpful to Mexican immigrants where she could place the kids during the day while she herself worked as a cleaning maid. He offered her the name and phone number of a *coyote* who could help her in the task of deceiving the U.S. border police.

The prospect of cleaning other people's dirt didn't appeal to La Llorona, but she was very hungry and so were the kids.

She decided to risk the mercy of strangers by traveling to Ciudad Juárez in whichever way she could.

Along the way people were helpful, but only to a certain degree. They offered an occasional *tortilla con frijoles* and gave them a ride on the back of a truck. The journey was extremely difficult. By the time they arrived, the second child, only three years old, had contracted diphtheria. La Llorona buried him in an unnamed pit somewhere in northeastern Nuevo León.

She decided not to give up, though. She contacted the *coyote* from a public phone, but he wanted to charge her $750. It was an astronomical amount; she didn't even have a small fraction of it. She begged him by telling the whole truth, that she had not even a roof where to stay overnight and that her children were dying of malnutrition. But the *coyote* hung up the phone. Many people came to him with the same litany.

On the street La Llorona's children were crying out loud. She began to ask for *una limoznita,* a small charity. After a while a passer-by gave her a few pesos. He whispered to her ear that she could get a few more by selling herself once or twice that night. She sobbed in desperation.

Then she saw a *feria,* a town fair. An idea crossed her mind. She would use the remaining money on amusement rides for her children, and while they were on them, she would run away. The thought overwhelmed her with remorse, but she had no other alternative.

And thus, when the kids were at *la rueda de la fortuna,* the Ferris wheel, La Llorona escaped without looking back. That morning, she had seen some Mexican peasants being taken in the direction of the border and she followed that same road. When she reached a fence, she jumped it and moved to a nearby river. Soon after she heard dogs barking and saw a helicopter.

A day later La Llorona was returned to Ciudad Juárez. In punishment for abandoning her children, the Almighty condemned her to wandering eternally in search of them.

Her shrieks are still heard at dawn in the city.

II
ROOTAS

SIMPLE VERSES

José Martí   **Translated by Manuel A. Tellechea**

José Martí (1852–95) was a famous journalist and activist who fought for the independence of his homeland, Cuba. He wrote a moving, compassionate poem for his son, entitled La edad de oro *(The Age of Gold). He was forced out of his country and lived for a time in the United States, where he wrote pieces about the Brooklyn Bridge and about a tragic earthquake in the city of Charleston, South Carolina, among other topics. His poems have been extremely popular. Portions of "Simple Verses" were set to music and are known as "Guantanamera." The following is a cluster of stanzas.*

A sincere man am I
From the land where palm trees grow,
And I want before I die
My soul's verses to bestow.

I'm a traveler to all parts,
And a newcomer to none;
I am art among the arts,
With the mountains I am one.

I know the strange names of willows,
And I can tell flowers with skill:
I know of lies that can kill,
And I know of sublime sorrows.

I have known a man to live
With a dagger at his side,

And never once the name give
Of she by whose hand he died.

All is beautiful and right,
All is like music and reason;
And like diamonds e'er this season,
All is coal before it's light.

I know when fools are laid to rest
Honor and tears will abound,
And that of all fruits, the best
Is left to rot in holy ground.

I have a white rose to tend
In July as in January;
I give it to the true friend
Who offers his frank hand to me.
And to the cruel one whose blows
Break the heart by which I live,
Thistle nor thorn do I give:
For him, too, I have a white rose.

VERSOS SENCILLOS

Yo soy un hombre sincero
De donde crece la palma,
Y antes de morirme quiero
Echar mis versos del alma

Yo vengo de todas partes,
Y hacia todas partes voy:

Arte soy entre las artes,
En los montes, monte soy.

Yo sé los nombres extraños
De las yerbas y las flores
Y de mortales engaños,
Y de sublimes dolores.

He visto vivir a un hombre
Con el puñal al costado,
Sin decir jamás el nombre
De aquella que lo ha matado.

Todo es hermoso y constante,
Todo es música y razón,
Y todo, como el diamante,
Antes que luz es carbón.

Yo sé que el necio se entierra
Con gran lujo y con gran llanto,—
Y que no hay fruta en la tierra
Como la del camposanto.

Cultivo una rosa blanca,
En julio como en enero,
Para el amigo sincero
Que me da su mano franca.
Y para el cruel que me arranca
El corazón con que vivo,
Cardo ni oruga cultivo:
Cultivo una rosa blanca.

DEPORTEE

Martin Hoffman and Woody Guthrie

*Woody Guthrie is best known for "This Land Is Your Land,"
and many of his songs capture the troubles of real people
trying to get by in tough times and in difficult situations.
He and Martin Hoffman wrote "Deportee," also known as
"Plane Wreck at Los Gatos." Linda Ronstadt made a popular recording of it. The tragedy is that it still describes
the lives Mexican migrant workers face in parts of America.*

The crops are in, the peaches are rotting
The oranges are piled in their creosote dumps
They're flying 'em back to the Mexican border
To pay all their money, to wade back again

My father's own father, he waded that river
They took all the money he made in his life
My brothers and sisters come work in the fruit fields
They rode in that truck till they took down and died

Good-bye to my Juan, good-bye Rosalita
Adios mis amigos, Jesús y María
You won't have a name when you ride the big airplane
All they will call you will be—deportee

Some of us are illegal and some of us ain't wanted
Our work contract's out and we're going to move on
Six hundred miles to the Mexican border
They treat us like rustlers, like outlaws, like thieves

The sky plane caught fire over Los Gatos canyon
A fireball of lightning shook all the fields

Who are all these friends all scattered like dry leaves
The radio said they're just deportees

Good-bye to my Juan, good-bye Rosalita
Adios mis amigos, Jesús y María
You won't have a name when you ride the big airplane
All they will call you will be—deportee.

DEPORTEE
Translated by Melquíades Sánchez

La cosecha 'tá lista, los duraznos se pudren
Las naranjas se apilan en canastos de aceitosos
Los vuelan de vuelta pa' la frontera con México
Pa' pagar sus deudas, pa' vadear otra vez

El padre de mi padre, él cruzó aquel río
Le quitaron la lana que hizo pa' comer
Mis hermanos y hermanas trabajan el llano
Montaron la troca hasta que la muerte se los llevó

Adiós a mi Juan, adiós Rosalita
Adiós mis amigos, Jesús y María
No tendrán siquiera un nombre cuando vuelen en avión
Solamente los llaman: deportee.

Algunos somos ilegales y algunos no somos bienvenidos
Acaba el contrato y vamos pa'lante
Seis mil millas hasta la frontera con México
Nos tratan como ganado, como bandidos y ladrones

Martin Hoffman and Woody Guthrie

El avión explotó por allá por Los Gatos Canyon
Los campos una bola de fuego estremeció
Quiénes son estos amigos, dispersos cual hojas secas
El radio dijo que nomás eran deportees.

Adiós a mi Juan, adiós Rosalita
Adiós mis amigos, Jesús y María
No tendrán siquiera un nombre cuando vuelen en avión
Solamente los llaman: deportee.

BLACK DANCE

Luis Palés Matos   **Translated by Julio Marzán**

Luis Palés Matos (1898–1959) was one of the most important poets in Puerto Rico. His book Tuntún de pasa y grifería *captures the African rhythms and sounds that are such an important strand of Caribbean history and life. His words become drum sounds where the beat is as important as the meaning:* "Calabó y bambú, bambú y calabó," *black wood and bamboo, bamboo and black wood.*

Black wood and bamboo.
Bamboo and black wood.
The Muckamuck he sings: too-coo-too.
The Muckamuck she sings: toe-co-toe.
It's the branding-iron sun's burn in Timbuktu.
It's the black dance danced on Fernando Po.
The mud-fest hog grunts: pru-pru-pru.
The bog-wet toad dreams: cro-cro-cro.
Black wood and bamboo.
Bamboo and black wood.

Juju strings strum a tempest of oos.
Tomtoms throb with dark bass ohs.
It's wave on wave of the black race in
The bloated rhythm of *mariyandá.*
Chieftains join the feasting now.
The Negress dances, dances entranced.
Black wood and bamboo.
Bamboo and black wood.
The He-Muckamuck sings: too-coo-too.
The She-muckamuck sings: toe-co-toe.

Red lands pass, bootblack islands:
Haiti, Martinique, Congo, Cameroon;
the *papiamiento* Antilles of rum,
the volcano's patois isles,
in rhythmic abandon
to dark-voweled song.

Black wood and bamboo.
Bamboo and black wood.
It's the branding-iron sun's burn in Timbuktu.
It's the black dance danced on Fernando Po.
It's the African soul that is throbbing in
The bloated rhythm of *mariyandá*.

Black wood and bamboo.
Bamboo and black wood.
The He-Muckamuck sings: too-coo-too
The She-Muckamuck sings: toe-co-toe.

DANZA NEGRA

Calabó y bambú.
Bambú y calabó.
El Gran Cocoroco dice: tu-cu-tu.
La Gran Cocoroca dice: to-co-to.
Es el sol de hierro que arde en Tombuktú.
Es la danza negra de Fernando Poo.
El cerdo en el fango gruñe: pru-pru-pru.
El sapo en la charca sueña: cro-cro-cro.
Calabó y bambú.
Bambú y calabó.

Rompen los junjunes en furiosa ú.
Los gongos trepidan con profunda ó.
Es la raza negra que ondulando va
en el ritmo gordo de mariyandá.
Llegan los botucos a la fiesta ya.
Danza que te danza la negra se da.

Calabó y bambú.
Bambú y calabó.
El Gran Cocoroco dice: tu-cu-tu.
La Gran Cocoroca dice: to-co-to.

Pasan tierras rojas, islas de betún:
Haití, Martinica, Congo, Camerún;
las papimientosas antillas del ron
y las patualesas islas del volcán,
que en el grave son
del canto se dan.

Calabó y bambú.
Bambú y calabó.
Es el sol de hierro que arde en Tombuktú.
Es la danza negra de Fernando Poo.
Es el alama africana que vibrando está,.
en el ritmo gordo dell mariyandá.

Calabó y bambú.
Bambú y calabó.
El Gran Cocoroco dice: tu-cu-tu.
La Gran Cocoroca dice: to-co-to.

TÍO PATRICIO

Jovita González

Jovita González (1904–83) was born in south Texas to a family of teachers. She loved the folk tales she heard on the U.S.-Mexican border and did much to preserve them and pass them on.

Every evening at dusk Tío Patricio was announced by the bleating of his unruly flock, which arrived enveloped in a cloud of dust. He was a giant dressed in a discarded soldier's uniform; however, his shoes and hat did not match his military array, for the former were rawhide *guaraches* and the latter a high, pointed, broad-brimmed Mexican felt *sombrero*. His black patriarchal beard contrasted with his cheeks, rosy and firm like a girl's. In fact, his complexion was the envy of all marriageable girls of the countryside. Not seldom a *señorita* braver than the rest ventured to ask, "What do you wash your face with, Tío?"

The reply was always the same, "God's water," meaning rain water. And in that semi-arid part of the country rain is rare, three or four times a year at most.

But that is another story.

You remember there was something peculiar about Tío Patricio. He always wore a hat in the summer, in winter, in fair weather and foul. Even at night he slept with it over his face so as to cover his head. He was rather sensitive about it too; no sooner would one of his ranch hands mention the word *head* or *hair* than the *pastor* silently disappeared. Of course, everyone wondered at this eccentricity but no one dared ask him to explain it. The most uncouth *vaquero* knows that no gentleman ever asks another anything concerning his personal appearance.

Sometime in November the master was to ship cattle, and new *vaqueros* were hired to help gather them. There was one in the outfit whom no one liked; he had snake-like beady black eyes that were as sly and crafty as a coyote's. Probably this started the men calling him "Coyote."

One evening, as customary, we were sitting around the kitchen fire telling yarns and singing. This particular night Coyote was telling about the ghosts that haunt El Blanco ranch. "Just about this time," he concluded in a haunting voice, "the moon shone from behind a cloud and I noticed that the ghost was as hairless as a pumpkin."

At this Tío Patricio jumped as if he had been stung by a scorpion and shot out of the kitchen with the rapidity of a hare when pursued by hounds.

"What's wrong with him?" asked Coyote. "He is a queer steer, ain't he? And, tell me, why does he always wear that steeple-like structure on his head? Do you dare to ask him why he never takes it off? I bet my *reata* against yours I'll do it. Who'll take my bid?"

No one said a word. Pancho changed the subject, for no one would hurt Tío Patricio's feelings willingly. We heard him fixing his bed in the bunk house. A mean look came into Coyote's eyes and I knew he meant to carry out his threat at the first opportunity.

"Come, boys," I said. "It is time to sleep. We have a hard day's work before us in the pasture tomorrow."

As we entered the house I saw Tío Patricio in bed with his hat over his face. Coyote went toward him.

"*Amigo,* you have forgotten to take off your hat." No answer. "I say, why don't you take it off, or shall I do it for you?"

He would have done it, too, had not Pancho grabbed him by the arm.

"Can't you see he is asleep," said Pancho, "and, what is more, you leave him alone. Do you hear?"

All expected trouble. Coyote measured Pancho with his eyes and, seeing the muscles of his arms and the determination on his face, skulked away.

Before daylight Tío Patricio was up and could be heard calling his dog in the corral. Not one word did anyone say about last night's episode, all hoping that Coyote would forget about it.

"I tell you what we'll do," he said the next morning as we were coming to the mess house for breakfast. "Suppose we recite the Rosary during the month of December; I am not much for religion but during this time I feel the need of it in my heart."

Although much surprised at the suggestion, all assented willingly, and I felt somewhat ashamed of my ill feelings toward him, and right then and there I made up my mind to like him.

Tío Patricio was not there during the services and all were surprised. He was not an overzealous religious man but we all knew his love and devotion for the Virgin.

Two weeks before Christmas, Coyote suggested we have *Las Posadas*. As everyone knows, these are the most solemn and beautiful services of the Christmas season. They are services which we who are all still Christians and speak God's own language hold every year in honor of the birth of the Christ Child.

"Since there is no church and no regular choir," continued Coyote, "I am going to ask the master to lend us a statue of the Virgin and we can have the services outside. You men will be arranged in groups so you can sing better; and another group representing Joseph and Mary go about asking for shelter and are refused everywhere. The person or group nearest the Virgin will take them in and with that the celebration will close."

"Can anyone as repulsive-looking as this man be capable of such beautiful ideas?" thought I. We were so busy rehearsing our hymns that we all forgot about Tío Patricio. All this time he had kept away from us and I noticed he looked worried. Probably, it was suggested, the goats were not doing so well this winter or he had lost some kids.

Christmas Eve finally came. About eight we went to the *portal,* the place of the celebration. Every man, conscious of his new shirt and rather sensitive about it, took his appointed seat. At a signal, the first group arose, went to the improvised altar, and sang the introduction:

Esta noche caballeros	This night gentlemen,
Es Noche de Navidad	Is Christmas Eve.
Parió la Virgen María	The Virgin Mary gave birth
Parió en humilde portal.	Under a humble roof.

The first group representing the holy Pilgrims started their pilgrimage:

Es José y María	This is Joseph and Mary
Su esposa amada	His beloved wife;
Es José y María	This is Joseph and Mary
Pidiendo posada.	Asking for shelter.

To which the addressed replied:

Mi casa es pequeña	My house is very small
No caben en ella.	There is no room for all.

And thus we went the rounds of all the groups. All this time I had been wondering who was to give lodging to the Pilgrims. Then my eyes fell on Tío Patricio. The man sat rigid, pale as the moon outside. On his face was the look of a haunted beast. And then it dawned on me. He was to sing the verse of acceptance. And he had to kneel bareheaded before the Virgin's altar. I knew Coyote was a despicable skunk, but I had not dreamed he would dare do a thing like this.

By this time all eyes were fixed on Tío Patricio. May I die before I again see anyone looking so abject and terrified. Have you ever seen a rabbit which, charmed by a snake, knows that soon it is to be devoured? That is the way Tío Patricio looked. I glanced toward Coyote; the grin of triumph on his ugly face made his namesake look handsome.

Then time came for Tío Patricio to start to sing. He got up and, walking with the steps of a somnambulist, approached the altar.

He knelt and took off his hat.

He was bald.

A dry, hoarse sob shook his mighty frame.

We left him there with his humiliation, alone with the mother of God.

KIPLING AND I

Jesús Colón

*Jesús Colón was born in Cayey, Puerto Rico. At the age of
seventeen he sailed on the SS Carolina to New York. He is
the author of A Puerto Rican in New York and Other
Sketches, a volume that includes many insightful anecdotes
about life in the United States as a Hispanic in the 1930s.
"Kipling and I" is about how a poem from an earlier time
and place speaks to a person dealing with present-day
realities.*

Sometimes I pass Debevoise Place at the corner of
Willoughby Street . . . I look at the old wooden house, gray
and ancient, the house where I used to live some forty years
ago . . .

My room was on the second floor at the corner. On hot
summer nights I would sit at the window reading by the electric
light from the street lamp, which was almost level with the
windowsill.

It was nice to come home late during the winter, look for
some scrap of old newspaper, some bits of wood, and a few
chunks of coal, and start a sparkling fire in the chunky four-
legged coal stove. I would be rewarded with an intimate
warmth as little by little the pigmy stove became alive, puffing
out its sides, hot and red, like the crimson cheeks of Santa
Claus.

My few books were in a soapbox nailed to the wall. But
my most prized possession in those days was a poem I had
bought in a five-and-ten-cent store on Fulton Street. (I wonder what has become of these poems, maxims, and sayings
of wise men that they used to sell at the five-and-ten-cent

37

stores?) The poem was printed on gold paper and mounted in a gilded frame ready to be hung in a conspicuous place in the house. I bought one of those fancy silken picture cords finishing in a rosette to match the color of the frame.

I was seventeen. This poem to me then seemed to summarize, in one poetical nutshell, the wisdom of all the sages that ever lived. It was what I was looking for, something to guide myself by, a way of life, a compendium of the wise, the true, and the beautiful. All I had to do was live according to the counsel of the poem and follow its instructions and I would be a perfect man—the useful, the good, the true human being. I was very happy that day forty years ago.

The poem had to have the most prominent place in the room. Where could I hang it? I decided that the best place for the poem was on the wall right by the entrance to the room. No one coming in or out would miss it. Perhaps someone would be interested enough to read it and drink the profound waters of its message . . .

Every morning as I prepared to leave, I stood in front of the poem and read it over and over again, sometimes half a dozen times. I let the sonorous music of the verse carry me away. I brought with me a handwritten copy as I stepped out every morning looking for work, repeating verses and stanzas from memory until the whole poem came to be part of me. Other days my lips kept repeating a single verse of the poem at intervals throughout the day.

In the subways I loved to compete with the shrill noises of the many wheels below by chanting the lines of the poem. People stared at me moving my lips as though I were in a trance. I looked back with pity. They were not so fortunate as I, who had as a guide to direct my life a great poem to make me wise, useful, and happy.

And I chanted:

If you can keep your head when all about you
Are losing theirs and blaming it on you . . .
If you can wait and not be tired by waiting,
Or being lied about, don't deal in lies,
Or being hated don't give way to hating . . .
If you can make one heap of all your winnings;
And risk it on one turn of pitch-and-toss,
And lose, and start again at your beginnings . . .

"If," by Kipling, was the poem. At seventeen, my evening prayer and my first morning thought. I repeated it every day with the resolution to live up to the very last line of that poem.

I would visit the government employment office on Jay Street. The conversations among the Puerto Ricans on the large wooden benches in the employment office were always on the same subjects. How to find a decent place to live. How they would not rent to Negroes and Puerto Ricans. How Negroes and Puerto Ricans were given the pink slips first at work.

From the employment office I would call door to door at the piers, factories, and storage houses in the streets under the Brooklyn and Manhattan Bridges. "Sorry, nothing today." It seemed to me that "today" was a continuation and combination of all the yesterdays, todays, and tomorrows.

From the factories I would go to the restaurants, looking for a job as a porter or a dishwasher. At least I would eat and be warm in a kitchen.

"Sorry" . . .

Sometimes I was hired at ten dollars a week, ten hours a day, including Sundays and holidays. One day off during the week. My work was that of three men: dishwasher, porter, busboy. And to clear the sidewalk of snow and slush "when you have nothing else to do." I was to be appropriately humble and grateful not only to the owner but to everybody else in the place.

If I rebelled at insults or at pointed innuendo or just the inhuman amount of work, I was unceremoniously thrown out and told to come "next week for your pay." "Next week" meant weeks of calling for the paltry dollars owed me. The owners relished this "next week."

I clung to my poem as to a faith. Like a potent amulet, my precious poem was clenched in the fist of my right hand inside my secondhand overcoat. Again and again I declaimed aloud a few precious lines when discouragement and disillusionment threatened to overwhelm me.

If you can force your heart and nerve and sinew
To serve your turn long after they are gone . . .

The weeks of unemployment and hard knocks turned into months. I continued to find two or three days of work here and there. And I continued to be thrown out when I rebelled at the ill treatment, overwork, and insults. I kept pounding the streets looking for a place where they would treat me half decently, where my devotion to work and faith in Kipling's poem would be appreciated. I remember the worn-out shoes I bought in a secondhand store on Myrtle Avenue at the corner of Adams Street. The round holes in the soles that I tried to cover with pieces of carton were no match for the frigid knives of unrelenting snow.

One night I returned late after a long day of looking for work. I was hungry. My room was dark and cold. I wanted to warm up my numb body. I lit a match and began looking for some scraps of wood and a piece of paper to start a fire. I searched all over the floor. No wood, no paper. As I stood up, the glimmering flicker of the dying match was reflected on the glass surface of the framed poem. I unhooked the poem from the wall. I reflected for a minute, a minute that felt like an eternity. I took the frame apart, placing the square glass upon the small table. I tore the gold paper upon which the poem was printed, threw its pieces inside the stove and, placing the small bits of wood from the frame on top of the paper, I lit it, adding soft and hard coal as the fire began to gain strength and brightness.

I watched how the lines of the poem withered into ashes inside the small stove.

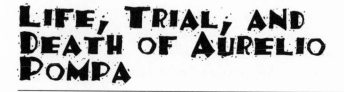

Life, Trial, and Death of Aurelio Pompa

Manuel Gamio

Anthropologist Manuel Gamio (1883–1960) spent a considerable portion of his time studying the life of the indigenous people of Mexico and documenting the path of Mexican immigrants to the United States. He collected this corrido *about Aurelio Pompa, a Mexican worker and a death-row inmate convicted of first-degree murder after he shot a carpenter. The* corrido *is a Mexican ballad that narrates a distinct plot. It is often used to describe the lives of folk heroes and villains. In Pompa's trial the prosecution argued that he and a coworker had an argument, after which Pompa went home, got a gun, and returned to kill the coworker. But the defense argued the opposite, and so did the Mexican community. They believed that Pompa had acted in self-defense after the carpenter had threatened him with a hammer. Pompa was eventually hanged.*

I'll tell you a sad story
of a Mexican who emigrated there—
Aurelio Pompa, so he was called,
our compatriot who died there

Out there in Caborca, in Sonora
the humble village where he was born,
"Come on, mother," he said one day,
"Over there, there are no revolutions."

"Good-bye, friends; good-bye María,"
he said to his betrothed very sadly.
"I promise you that I will return soon,
So we can get married, God willing."

"Good-bye, Aurelio," said the girl,
and she went sobbing to pray.
"Look after him, Virgin Mary,
I have a foreboding he will not come back."

His priest and his friends
along with his sweetheart
talked and begged poor Aurelio
not to leave his native village.

Such advice was useless,
so were his mother's pleas.
"Let's go, mother, over there is the dollar.
I swear I'll earn a lot of them."

Four years ago in the month of May
the two of them went to California
and on the very same date
he died there in prison through misfortune.

A carpenter who was very strong
struck the poor young fellow cruelly.
Aurelio Pompa swore to be revenged
for those blows he had received.

Filled with rage he told his mother about it.
The poor old woman advised him,
"*Por Dios,* forget it, dear son."
And good Aurelio forgave him.

But one afternoon, while working
with three friends at the railroad station
the carpenter came to mock him
and aroused poor Pompa.

The three friends advised him
to leave him alone and go his way,
but the carpenter, with a hammer,
very offensively threatened him.

Then Pompa, seeing the danger,
fired in self-defense
with a revolver and face to face
as a man he killed him.

The case in court, the jury arrived,
and the Yankee people sentenced him.
"The death penalty," they all demanded,
and the lawyer did not object.

Twenty thousand signatures
asked the governor for pardon,
all the newspapers asked for it too,
and even Obregón sent a message.

All was useless; the societies
all united, asked his pardon.
His poor mother, half dead already,
also went to see the governor.

"Farewell, my friends, farewell, my village.
Dear mother, cry no more.
Tell my race not to come here.
For they will suffer here; there's no pity here."

The jailer asked him:
"Were you Spanish?" And he answered,
"I'm Mexican and proud of it,
although they deny me a pardon."

This is the story of a compatriot,
who four years ago arrived there,
unfortunately on the same date
died dreadfully in prison.

VIDA, PROCESO Y MUERTE DE AURELIO POMPA

Voy a contarles la triste historia
de un mexicano que allá emigró
Aurelio Pompa, así se llamaba,
el compatriota que allí murió.

Allá en Caborca que es de Sonora,
el pueblo humilde donde nació,
"Vámonos, madre," le dijo un día
que allá no existe revolución.

"Adiós, amigos, adiós, María,"
dijo a la novia con gran dolor,
yo te prometo que pronto vuelvo,
para casarnos, mediante Dios.

Adiós, Aurelio, dijo la novia,
que sollozando se fue a rezar
cuídalo mucho, Virgen María,
que yo presiento no volverá.

El señor cura y sus amigos,
junto a la novia fueron a hablar,
a suplicarle al pobre Aurelio
que no dejara el pueblo natal.

Fueron inútiles tantos consejos
también los ruegos de su mamá
vámonos, madre, que allá está el dólar
y mucho, juro, que ha de ganar.

El mes de mayo de hace cuatro años
a California fueron los dos
y por desgracia en la misma fecha
en una cárcel allá murió.

Un carpintero que era muy fuerte,
al pobre joven muy cruel golpeó,
y Aurelio Pompa juró vengarse
de aquellos golpes que recibió.

Lleno de rabia contó a la madre
y la pobre anciana le aconsejó
"por Dios, olvida, hijo querido,"
y el buen Aurelio le perdonó.

Pero una tarde, que trabajaba,
con tres amigos en la estación
el carpintero pasó burlando
y al pobre Pompa le provocó.

Los tres amigos le aconsejaban
que lo dejara y fuera con Dios
y el carpintero, con un martillo
muy injurioso lo amenazó.

Entonces Pompa, viendo el peligro,
en su defensa le disparó
con el revólver y cara a cara,
como los hombres él lo mató.

Vino la causa, llegó el jurado
y el pueblo yanqui lo sentenció.
"Pena de muerte" pidieron todos,
y el abogado no protestó.

Veinte mil firmas de compatriotas
perdón pidieron al gobernador
toda la prensa también pedía
y hasta un mensaje mandó Obregón.

Todo fue inútil, las sociedades,
todas unidas pedían perdón.
La pobre madre, ya casi muerta,
también fue a ver al gobernador.

"Adiós, amigos, adiós, mi pueblo,
Querida madre, no llores más,
dile a mi raza que ya no venga
que aquí se sufre que no hay piedad."

El carcelero le preguntaba;
"¿español eres?" y él contestó
"soy mexicano y orgullo serlo
aunque me nieguen a mí el perdón."

Esta es la historia de un compatriota
que hace cuatro años allí llegó
y por desgracia en la misma fecha
en una carcél muy mal murió.

III
D'ATRÁS Y
D'ALANTE

FRUTAS

Ricardo Pau-Llosa

Ricardo Pau-Llosa is a poet and Latin American art critic born in Havana in 1954. His poetry captures the way Cuba is such a vivid part of the life of Cubans in America, even though they may never see it again.

Growing up in Miami any tropical fruit I ate
could only be a bad copy of the Real Fruit of Cuba.
Exile meant having to consume false food,
and knowing it in advance. With joy
my parents and grandmother would encounter
Florida-grown mameyes and caimitos at the market.
At home they would take them out of the American bag
and describe the taste that I and my older sister
would, in a few seconds, be privileged to experience
for the first time. We all sat around the table
to welcome into our lives this football-shaped,
brown fruit with the salmon-colored flesh
encircling an ebony seed. "Mamey,"
my grandmother would say with a confirming nod,
as if repatriating a lost and ruined name.
Then she bent over the plate,
slipped a large slice of mamey into her mouth,
then straightened in her chair and, eyes shut,
lost herself in comparison and memory.
I waited for her face to return with a judgment.
"No, not even the shadow of the ones back home."
She kept eating, more calmly,
and I began tasting the sweet and creamy pulp,
trying to raise the volume of its flavor

so that it might become a Cuban mamey. "The good
Cuban mameyes didn't have primaveras," she said
after the second large gulp, knocking her spoon
against a lump in the fruit and winking.
So at once I erased the lumps in my mental mamey.
I asked her how the word for "spring"
came to signify "lump" in a mamey. She shrugged.
"Next you'll want to know how we lost a country."

FRUTAS

Criándome en Miami, cualquier fruta tropical
que comiera sólo podía ser una copia degradada
de la Verdadera Fruta de Cuba.
Vivir en el exilio significaba la obligación
de consumir comida falsa y saberlo
por adelantado. Con alegría mis padres
y abuela descubrían mameyes y caimitos
cosechados en la Florida en el mercado.
Cuando llegaban a casa los sacaban
de la bolsa americana y describirían
el sabor que yo y mi hermana mayor
tendríamos, en unos instantes, el privilegio
de probar por primera vez. Todos nos sentamos
alrededor de la mesa de comer
para darle la bienvenida a nuestas vidas
a esta fruta con forma de fútbol
marrón por fuera y con pulpa color salmón
envolviendo una semilla de ébano.
"Mamey," diría mi abuela moviendo la cabeza
en afirmación, como si estuviera repatriando
un nombre perdido y arruinado.

Se dobló sobre el plato y deslizó
entre sus dientes una tajada de mamey.
Entonces se enderezó en su silla y,
con ojos cerrados, se perdió en comparaciones
y recuerdos. Esperé a que su cara regresara
con un veredicto. "No, ni la sombra
de aquellos mameyes." Siguió comiendo,
con más calma, y fue entonces que empecé
a probar la carne dulce y cremosa del mamey,
tratando de subir el volumen de su sabor
para que se hiciera, para mí, un mamey cubano.
"Los buenos mameyes cubanos no tenían primaveras,"
dijo despues de tragar otro pedazo
mientras golpeaba un bulto en la fruta
y guiñaba un ojo. Inmediatamente borré
todos los bultos de mi mamey mental.
Le pregunté cómo fue que la palabra "primavera"
vino a significar un bulto en un mamey.
Se encojió de hombros. "Y ahora vas
a querer saber cómo pudimos perder un país."

RICOCHET

Virgil Suárez

Virgil Suárez was born in Havana in 1962. His family left the island in 1970 and settled in Spain, then moved to the United States. In books such as Spared Angola *he reminisces on his childhood. "Ricochet" is about a friendship between a pair of boys living under communism, where the stresses the families face from government are expressed in horrifying ways. The story, like the poems "Frutas" and "Sugarcane," is set against a Cuban background—a Cuba of tragedy and nostalgia.*

I'm working the rubber band made from a long strip I cut from my bicycle tire's inner tube. The black, powdery residue of the rubber leaves fingerprints on the surface where I'm doing the work. Trying not to get a tear in the rubber. This is the second time I try. I'm hiding in the back yard, by the sink and faucet where my mother usually does the wash, out of reach so nobody sees me, nobody bothers me. I'm thinking I'm going to have the meanest, bestest slingshot musket in the neighborhood. I'm going to shoot lizards' heads off with bottle caps. Fermán, my black friend at school, showed me the original drawing of the thing itself. I copied it and now I'm building it back here by the chicken coops, using my father's hammer, scissors, and a few furniture tacks I removed from the bottom of the sofa.

Nobody will miss them, and nobody can see the flap of material hanging loose like a dog's ear.

The rubber holds, dangles around my hands like a pair of black snakes. Fine rubber. The best, which I took from the front wheel of my bicycle. I put the tire back on so my father wouldn't see the thing missing. Only a flat tire, and any bike can have that. I just won't ride it, and if they ask me to I'll say I don't feel like it. My father's been gone for two or three days now. The secret police, as my mother called the two civilian-dressed men, came and arrested my father. I'm here in the house with my grandmother.

I haven't seen my parents in a few days.

The G-Dos, secret police, came for my dissident father. My father, the gusano—this much I know is true.

Every time I glance over at my bicycle with its flat front tire, leaning against the gate that separates the chickens from the rabbits, I think of my father. He stands in line for days to get me this bicycle, and I know he'll be angry if he ever finds out. My grandmother tells me he'll be back home any minute now, but we haven't heard from him or my mother. The neighbors keep coming by to talk to my grandmother, find out what happened. The next door neighbors, Miriam and her son Chichi, come by and I almost show Chichi my slingshot musket, but then I think better of it. If I show it around everyone will ask questions. They will glimpse its beauty soon enough.

It's almost done, and I've collected enough bottle caps on the way home from school and back to have a real shoot-out war. Everyone in the neighborhood has slingshots, including Chichi, but nobody has this one. I hold the 2 x 2 piece of wood in my hand, feel its weight on my fingers. I sanded it down on the sides real smooth because I didn't want to get any more splinters in the tips of my fingers. I plan to paint it red or black, like a real pirate's musket I've seen on TV.

My grandmother, who cooks in the kitchen, keeps poking her head out of the kitchen entrance to ask if I need anything. I've been out here for a long time, long enough to get used to the thick, musky smell of the chickens. A rooster hops up to the fence and eyes me the way chickens do. Turns this side first, then the other. I aim the thing at it and pretend I slice its head off. One clean shot. I want to line up the trigger with the front muzzle. I've cut two feet of rubber for each side. I load one side, then the other. Each side holds three bottle cap back-ups, so that I could reload real fast.

Then Ricardito, my friend from the other side of the fence, shows up on top of the fence between his house and mine. I can't hide the musket fast enough.

"What are you doing?" he asks and licks his lips. He always licks his lips when he's nervous.

"Hey, not much." I want to tell him not now, that I don't want to play. But he looks like he isn't going to jump down and leave me alone, so I glare up at him. He's older by two years, but everything we play I always beat him. My mother once told me the story of how when I was three I peed in my bottle and gave Ricardito it to drink from, told him it was delicious orange juice. I don't remember doing it, but my mother says I did.

"Wanna play ball?" he says, his dirty hands gripping the cement at the top of the cinder block wall. His father always threatens to stick broken pieces of bottles up there so we won't jump the fence so often. Ricardito broke his arm once when we used to walk it up and down, balancing ourselves up there like in tightrope acts.

"Not right now."

"Has your father come back?"

My father, the traitor. My father the counter-revolutionary.

"No, not yet." I feel the rubber bands underneath my thighs as I squat over them so Ricardito won't see them. He's my best friend, but once he sees something of mine he can't stop asking questions.

"My father says they can keep him in prison for good," he says. I don't want to think about my father, so I don't say anything.

"They'll make him cut sugar cane." Once you get him going, he can never stop. There's no way to do it unless you get his mind off on something else. I don't because I don't want him to start asking me questions about what I'm doing.

He sits there and dangles his legs over the side. His scuffed shoes scrape against the cement. I can see the worn sole on one shoe, and the crack in the other. He isn't wearing socks and his ankles and calves are riddled with mosquito bites, whole constellations of them, some red, others crusted over with purple scabs. The sores never go away because he loves to pick off the scabs and look at them real close. He told me once he saves them all in a jar, and I believe him. I believe anything he says when it concerns his body.

One time when we were alone in the house, he called me into the bathroom where I had found him with a bloody mouth. He kept spitting up blood and saliva, and when I asked him what had happened he showed me his loose tooth. He'd pulled on a tooth long enough to jiggle it loose, and now his gums were bleeding. This was a permanent tooth too.

Whenever he smiles he's got a gap right there. His parents refuse to take him to the dentist, and his father beat him silly because of it.

"What are you going to do if your father doesn't come back?" Ricardito asked.

"He'll come back."

"Not if they don't want him to. You think they'll kill him?"

"My grandmother says he will."

Ricardito hates my grandmother because she always chases him away with a broom. She calls him the little animal, the little pest. "Animalito," she screams at him. "Salte de aquí! Vete ya!"

He sticks his big, candy-stained tongue out at her.

Once he fell as he ran and scraped his knees, but he didn't cry. I thought of him that night, in bed, waiting for the blood to dry, crust up into giant scabs so he could start digging his dirty nails underneath. He says that if you look at the underside of a scab, you can see the patterns of skin as it heals, like when you cut a tree down and count the rings to see how old the tree is. Except his never heal. He bleeds onto his bed sheets, and his mother never asks why, or where the blood comes from. His mother can't see very well. She wears glasses thicker than the bottoms of bottles.

When I realize Ricardito isn't going to go away, I figure I could ask him to get me something. I need a big nail for a trigger. "Does your father have a nail I can use?" I ask.

"What do you want a nail for?"

"I can't tell you. Does he have one?"

"He might. It depends."

"If you get me one I will tell you."

He stares at me with his eyebrows furrowed, like he always does because half of the things I say he never believes, and also because he's too used to my fooling him and pulling his leg all the time. Maybe there's some truth to the bottle of my urine he drank.

No use. I see it in his eyes. He's in one of those lazy moods. I can tell. He doesn't feel like jumping down. What can I do?

"If I tell you what I'm doing," I tell him, "do you promise not to tell?"

"I might, might not."

"Mierda."

He looks hurt because he never likes it when I call him shit. I feel sorry for him all of a sudden.

"All right."

"OK," he says.

"Can't you tell what it is?"

"A slingshot."

"Better than that."

"Where did you get the rubber bands?"

I don't answer, just shrug.

He jumps down now, his feet landing flat and square by the mound of bottle caps. He lands on it and crushes a few. Startled, the chickens flutter into a ruckus.

"Take it easy," I say. "Look where you're jumping."

He apologizes, but it's no use. I can tell. He wants to know more than ever what it is I'm building.

I show him. "See, it's a musket, a rifle, a machine gun of bottle caps."

I explain how I plan to shoot bottle caps at lizards, at birds, at anything I find.

Already he's all hands. I hate that about him, his groping around with his dirty hands and fingernails. He's about to pull on the rubber bands, stretch them for the first time, and I yank them out of his hands.

If I found the nail, and I put the thing together, I could convince Ricardito to play firing squad. I heard one of my parents' friends mention something about it once. One of my father's friends, Guillermo, who rode the motorcycle—he rode me around a few times, up and down the street, what a great thrill—and he never came home one afternoon. Guillermo was a gusano, my parents always called him. Gusano means worm, maggot. I found out it means dissident, counter-revolutionary, the kind that could get you killed or disappeared in Cuba. When my father called Guillermo gusano, he always shot back: "It takes one to know one." And both he and my father laughed real hard.

I can play firing squad with Ricardito, yeah.

We look around the chicken coop and rabbit hutches until I find the right nail, then I pull it out slowly. With one knee on the ground and Ricardito breathing over my head, I straighten it out. It has a wide enough head for what I need. The wide head holds the bottle cap under the pressure from the rubber band, and then I can flick it easy like flipping a coin up in the air.

I measure one last time, still making sure that Ricardito doesn't touch any more of the bottle caps—I had them counted—and hammer the nail into place.

"It's done," I say and hold up my brand-new musket. "Look how beautiful."

"Can I hold it?" Ricardito licks his dry, cracked lips.

"Not yet," I say and turn away from him until I can load it properly.

The rubber bands stretch just fine, with plenty of tension. I imagine the bottle caps going fast and hard, easily lobbing off the head of any lizard, frog, snake. Great, I think and feel the excitement in my throat.

The rubber band hugs the first three caps, then I load the second one, another three. It's ready.

I want to shoot it before my grandmother hears us.

"Stand against the wall, just straight like that."

"Why?"

"Just do it," I tell him.

He backs up against the dirty lime walls in the patio of our house in Habana. A little nervous, he fidgets. His shoulders slump, his hands flutter about in and out of his pockets.

"Move back more, right up against the wall."

Then I think of the perfect idea. I blindfold him to make it look real enough. Then Ricardito can't see, and he won't know how the thing works, and he'll be too scared to want to shoot it. I figure I could aim for his gut, or his hands.

I find a rag by the sink, take it and fold it over his eyes.

"I can't see," he says.

"That's the idea." I turn him a few times like he's going to beat up a piñata or pin the tail on the donkey.

Then I back him up against the wall. I decide now that since his eyes are covered he won't have to face the wall. He won't know when I fire. He'll only hear and feel the bottle caps bite into his skin, and if I miss, he'll hear them buzz past his ears.

He stands there blindfolded, his head tilted upward as though he's trying to sneak a peek.

I walk back counting twenty paces. I hold my musket between my legs, pull back on the rubber bands, load, and aim.

"What is this called?"

"Firing squad," I say and close one eye.

I bite down on my tongue as I concentrate, all along thinking of the bottle caps as real bullets. The machine gun in my hand. Ricardito isn't my friend anymore, but my father. I hear my father's voice talking about how he wants to leave the country, take me out of it before the government brainwashes me into thinking my own father is my enemy.

My father, tall and thin, learns to study the bullet marks on the walls. He says they tell tragic stories. A whole calligraphic record of those who've been shot, disappeared, for telling the truth about corrupt governments.

An old-fashioned firing squad like the Spanish used with their shiny muskets. With their conquests. With all that rancor and rage in their hearts.

"What's taking so long?" Ricardo speaks and breaks my concentration.

I take aim. My trigger finger trembles against the nail, then steadies, and I open fire.

Coca-Cola and Coco Frío

Martín Espada

Through his poetry Martín Espada gives voice to Puerto Ricans who live in the United States. Born in 1957, he is a former tenant lawyer and a teacher. His poetry is incisive and compassionate at once.

On his first visit to Puerto Rico,
island of family folklore,
the fat boy wandered
from table to table
with his mouth open.
At every table, some great-aunt
would steer him with cool spotted hands
to a glass of Coca-Cola.
One even sang to him, in all the English
she could remember, a Coca-Cola jingle
from the forties. He drank obediently, though
he was bored with this potion, familiar
from soda fountains in Brooklyn.

Then, at a roadside stand off the beach, the fat boy
opened his mouth to coco frío, a coconut
chilled, then scalped by a machete
so that a straw could inhale the clear milk.
The boy tilted the green shell overhead
and drooled coconut milk down his chin;
suddenly, Puerto Rico was not Coca-Cola
or Brooklyn, and neither was he.

For years afterward, the boy marveled at an island
where the people drank Coca-Cola
and sang jingles from World War II
in a language they did not speak,
while so many coconuts in the trees
sagged heavy with milk, swollen
and unsuckled.

Coca-Cola y Coco Frío
Translated by Maribel Pintado-Espiet

En su primera visita a Puerto Rico,
isla del folclor familiar,
el niño gordo se paseaba
de mesa en mesa
con la boca abierta.
En cada mesa, una tía abuela
con manos frescas y manchadas
le guiaba hasta un vaso de Coca-Cola.
Otra hasta le cantó, con todo el inglés
que recordaba, un anuncio de Coca-Cola
de los años cuarenta. Obediente, bebió, pese
a su aburrimiento con el elixir conocido
de las fuentes de soda de Brooklyn.

Luego, en un ventorrillo cerca de la playa, el niño gordo
abrió la boca al coco frío, un coco helado
que el machete había descabellado
para que una pajilla pudiera aspirar la leche clara.
El niño inclinó el verde carapacho sobre su cabeza
dejando que la leche de coco le corriera barbilla abajo.
Súbitamente, Puerto Rico no era Coca-Cola
ni era Brooklyn y él, tampoco era.

*Años más tarde, el niño se maravillaba ante una isla
donde la gente tomaba Coca-Cola
cantando anuncios de la 2da Guerra Mundial
en un lenguaje que no hablaban,
mientras que en las palmeras tantísimos cocos
colgaban, cargados de leche, hinchados,
sin amamantar.*

THE JEWISH CEMETERY IN GUANABACOA

Ruth Behar

Ruth Behar was born in Cuba in 1956 into a Jewish family. When Fidel Castro came to power, she left the island and was educated in the United States, where eventually she became an anthropologist. This poem is a journey into the past of the Jewish community in Cuba. Behar travels, her camera in hand, in search of the tomb of a relative.

Outside of Havana
are the Jews
who won't leave Cuba
until the coming
of the Messiah.

There is the grave
of Sender Kaplan's father
a rabbi's grave
encircled by an iron gate
shaded by a royal palm.

There is the grave
in Hebrew letters
that speak Spanish
words of love and loss.
Ay kerida, why so soon?

There is the grave
with a crooked

Star of David.
There is the grave
crumbled like feta.

I go searching
for the grave
of my cousin
who was too rich
to die.

I despair.
I've promised a picture
to my aunt and uncle.
They're rich now in Miami
but not a penny for Fidel.

And then I find it—
the grave of Henry Levin
who died of leukemia
at age twelve
and money couldn't save him.

Poor boy,
he got left behind
with the few living Jews
and all the dead ones
for whom the doves pray.

I reach for my camera
but the shutter won't click.
Through ninety long miles
of burned bridges I've come
and Henry Levin won't smile.

I have to return another day
for Henry Levin's grave
with a friend's camera.
Mine is useless for the rest
of the trip, transfixed, dead.

Only later I learn
why Henry Levin
rejected me
a latecomer
to his grave.

My aunt and uncle were wrong.
Henry Levin is not abandoned.
Your criada, the black woman
who didn't marry to care for him,
tends his grave.

Tere tells me she can't forget
Henry, he died in her arms.
Your family left you, cousin,
so thank God for a black woman
who still visits your little bones.

EL CEMENTERIO MACABEO EN GUANABACOA

En las afueras de La Habana
están los judíos
que jamás se irán de Cuba
hasta que no llegue
el Mesías.

Allí está la tumba
del padre de Sender Kaplan
la tumba de un rabino
rodeada de una cerquilla de hierro
gozando de la sombra de una palma real.

Allí está la tumba
con sus letras hebreas
que hablan en español
de korazones tristes.
Ay kerida, ¿por qué te fuiste?

Allí está la tumba
con su Estrella de David
toda torcida.
Allí está la tumba
gratinada como un queso feta.

Yo busco
la tumba
de un primo
que era demasiado rico
para morir.

Me desespero.
Le he prometido una foto
a mi tía y mi tío
que se hicieron hasta más ricos en Miami
pero ni un centavo a Fidel.

Y de repente la encuentro—
la tumba de Henry Levin
que se murió de leucemia
a los doce años
y no pudieron salvarlo con dinero.

Pobrecito
lo dejaron atrás
con los pocos judíos vivos
y todos los muertos
a quienes les rezan las palomas.

Subo la cámara a mis ojos
y no me deja disparar.
Noventa millas de puentes quemados
he venido viajando
y mi primo no quiere sonreír.

Tengo que regresar otro día
para llevarme la tumba de Henry Levin
con la cámara de una amiga.
La mía no se recupera en todo el viaje,
se paraliza, muere.

Después entiendo
por qué Henry Levin
me rechaza
por llegar tarde
a su tumba.

Mi tía y mi tío estaban equivocados.
Su hijo no está abandonado.
La criada que tuvieron, la mujer negra
que no se casó por estar cuidándolo
no deja de acariciar su tumba.

Tere me dice que ella no se puede olvidar
de Henry porque murió en sus brazos.
Tu familia allí te dejó, primo,
así que dale gracias a Dios
que una mujer negra visita tus huesitos.

CORAZÓN DEL CORRIDO

Pat Mora

Pat Mora is a poet who uses words to explore the senses. She was born in El Paso, Texas, and has written many books for young children and middle graders, such as My Own True Name: New and Selected Poems for Young Adults, 1984–1999. *This* corrido *was composed in Spanish by the author to pay homage to her father and his culture. To translate it into English would defeat its original intention.*

1
En la frontera de Tejas,
miren lo que ha sucedido,
venían los mexicanos
buscaban lo prometido.

2
En mil novecientos quince,
de Chihuahua Moras llegaban,
buscaban paz pa' sus hijos,
el Paso Norte mudaban.

3
Venía Raúl Antonio,
llegó de niño chiquito,
a las siete ya trabajaba,
llechero con caballito.

4
Buscaba otro trabajo,
periódicos él vendía
despúes de ir a la escuela
tantas tareas tenía.

5
De chico iba a los pleitos,
—Soy de la prensa, decía,
en periódicos se sentaba,
gran boxeadores veía.

6
Jugetón desde muy joven,
a su hermana asustaba,
vestido en sábana blanca,
como espanto gritaba.

7
Su padre, sastre paciente,
su madre nunca paraba,
esa familia tan grande,
Raúl lo necesitaba.

8
Decía Raúl Antonio,
y sin pistola en la mano,
y sin caballo melado,
—Soy luchador mexicano.

9
Un hombre bien aplicado,
gerente pues lo nombraban,
su sueldo daba a su madre,
amigos lo admiraban.

10
Pero llegaban los güeros,
que ojos malos le daban.
—Jamás podrán insultarme,
¡Adiós! Ya no lo abusaban.

11
—¿Qué haré? Pensaba ese joven,
cuando lavaba su coche,
—Te ocupo, dijo un viandante.
—Iré al taller día y noche.

12
Los lentes él pulía,
y las medidas tomaba.
—¡Muchachos, prisa! gritaba.
Ni pa' comidas paraba.

13
A veces dando un paseo,
bonita joven veía,
sentada frente a su casa,
—¡Qué linda! Raúl decía.

14
—Con esa voy a casarme.
pronto con ella salía,
mandaba muchos regalos,
y ella se sonreía.

15
Esposo de bella Estrella,
de piedra casa fincaron,
y cuatro hijos tuvieron,
los cuatro bien educaron.

16
Fue dueño de su negocio,
al pobre siempre ayudaba,
por años de día y noche,
los lentes él trabajaba.

17
Decía Raúl Antonio,
y sin pistola en la mano,
—Yo cuidaré a mi familia,
Soy luchador mexicano.

18
Al fin las cuentas montaban,
se fue buscando dinero,
a Houston, Gallup, Califas,
se mudó entre el güero.

19
Jugetón desde muy joven,
con nietos siempre guasaba,
les daba pues su domingo,
y luego les pellizcaba.

20
¡Ay! Murió en California
y sin pistola en la mano,
y sin caballo melado,
gran luchador mexicano.

21
Aquí se acaba el corrido,
Y como él lucharemos,
ya con ésta me despido,
¡Ay, Papá! te cantaremos.

—for my father

 STARFISH

Dionisio D. Martínez

Dionisio D. Martínez, born in Cuba in 1956, lives in Tampa, Florida, where he works in the Poets-in-the-Schools Program. In this enthralling poem, the sky becomes a mirror in which the sea and the earth are reflected.

That's not rain; it's a starfish constellation falling. When we go fishing we just hold out

Our hands like nets. I wash them in salt
And they turn into islands. Trees sprout

from my lifelines. They taught me that clouds
are vapor that escapes from the water and rises

only to fall again. Like most island stories, this one
goes unquestioned. We will pry

open your starstruck, star-filled hands one
day. Let them clutch a little light while they

can. Clouds are helium islands, floating,
unbelievable as the sky itself. Let this be

your story, your amulet of words, the only magnet
that guides your compass across a starless continent.

—for Jessica Marie Cason

Dionisio D. Martínez

ESTRELLAS DE MAR

Eso no es lluvia, es una constelación de estrellas de
mar desplomándose. Cuando vamos de pesca, tendemos

las manos como redes. Las lavo con sal
y se vuelven islas. Árboles brotan

de las líneas que cuentan mi vida. Me habían enseñado
que las nubes son vapor que se escapa del agua y se eleva

pare volver al agua. Como es de esperar en una isla, este
cuento se toma como un hecho. Abriremos un día

a la fuerza tus manos asombradas, llenas de
estrellas. Deja que atrapen un poco de luz mientras

puedan. Las nubes son islas de helio que flotan
inconcebiblemente, come el cielo. Deja que este sea

tu relato, tu amuleto de palabras, el único imán
que guía tu compás a través de un continente sin estrellas.

—para Jessica Marie Cason

76

OY! WHAT A HOLIDAY!

Ilan Stavans

Ilan Stavans grew up in a Jewish family in Mexico, speaking several languages. He is fascinated by how a language both hides and reveals the person who uses it, so that a person who is bilingual has two masks. He has written on this issue in an autobiography, On Borrowed Words.

Hanukkah in Distrito Federal was a season of joy. The week-long festival of light was celebrated at home and in school and, indirectly, in our gentile neighborhood where it was part of the season of *posadas.* Hanukkah almost always fell near Christmas, so many of my holiday memories blend Judas Maccabee with piñatas filled with oranges, *colación,* and bite-sized pieces of sugar cane. In our Yiddish school, we performed humorous *schpiels,* reenacting the plight of the Hasmoneans who waged a guerrilla war in Palestine in 165 B.C. when the Syrian ruler Antiochus IV desecrated Jerusalem's Holy Temple.

In my mind, the event was a mirror of the kind of uprising South American left-wing *comandantes* were famous for orchestrating in Bolivia, El Salvador, and Nicaragua. I would imagine the Hasmoneans as freedom fighters dressed in army fatigues and using Uzis. In fact, I remember playing Antiochus once—a role I thoroughly enjoyed—and also once Judas's father, Mattathias of Modin, a man with a beard very much like Fidel Castro's. As Antiochus I dressed like a Spanish conquistador and, simulating the voice of Presidente Luis Echeverría Alvarez, I pretended to conquer the temple, designed after the pyramid of the sun of Teotihuacán. At the end of the play we all sang classic Hebrew songs like "Hanerot Hallalu," "Maoz Tsur," and "Hava Narima," but in the style of ranchero ballads, sounding like El Mariachi Vargas de Tecalitlán, and using verbal puns to satirize Mexican and Israeli political events. In the early evening, my parents would give me and my siblings our presents (I still remember a beautiful *títere,* a puppet of a humble *campesino* with huge mustache, a bottle in one hand and a pistol in the other) and then we would light another one of the candles in the menorah, placing the candelabra in the dining room window sill.

Occasionally, our extended family gathered at my grandmother's house in Colonia Hipódromo, where the cousins sat in circles spinning the dreidl, a little top on which we gambled our Hanukkah money. (I remember that no matter how much I prayed for a miracle like the one that swept the Maccabees to redemption, I would never manage to get the winning number and so, at the end of the evening, I would be left with no assets to speak of and a bad temper.) After the game, as we would on other Jewish holidays like Rosh Hashanah and Yom Kippur, we ate a Mexican meal, with Grandma's inevitable *pescado a la veracruzana,* chicken soup with *kneidlach,* the over-fried latkes accompanied by *mole poblano* and applesauce. By way of dessert, we would have delicious pastries that attempted to invoke the baking style of Eastern European Jewry but were really indigenous *bizcochos.*

As if this were not enough, at the end of the day we were often invited to join neighbors in their *posadas* and at this point, as I recall, numerous theological questions about the meaning of Hanukkah and Judaism in general were asked by our gentile aquaintances:

"Why eight candles?" someone would ask.

"Well, it's because of a *milagro,* a miracle—"

"Gosh, you guys believe in miracles? The only miracle that ever happened was the one that gave life to our Lord Jesus."

Silence.

"Did you guys really kill Jesus Christ? Do you consider Him the Messiah?"

Suddenly, my mind would go blank. "You mean us, personally?"

"Do you Jews consider Him the Messiah?"

"Do you know what the Immaculate Conception is?"

Searching for replies to these queries would leave me with a bizarre, uncomfortable aftertaste. No, I had not killed Jesus, and neither did we consider him a messiah. Our gentile friends never took our answers at face value. Their faces betrayed their puzzlement. They liked us, no doubt, and perhaps a few even loved us—but we were clearly from another planet.

While being different to other people in the neighborhood was no doubt discomfiting, I eventually learned to enjoy it. I came to realize that, like me, my parents and teachers had been asked the exact same set of questions when they were little, and that they, as much as my siblings and I, were part of a culture that had learned to live at peace and with respect in different societies. As a group we have been nurtured and have become stronger by what each environment has offered us, and, in return, we have paid back by offering our own answers—and also some questions—to those around us.

Sweet Fifteen

Rolando Hinojosa-Smith

Rolando Hinojosa-Smith was born in Mercedes, Texas, in 1929. In his books he explores the life of Klail City, an imaginary region in the Rio Grande Valley he himself invented. He does this by offering anecdotes, interviews, and discussions with its people. "Sweet Fifteen" show-cases the traditional quinceañera *parties in the Valley.*

I was thirteen years old and much too short to be dancing with a fifteen-year-old, but the occasion was her debut, she was fifteen, and it was her *quinceañera* party. This was the mid-forties, in Mercedes in the Rio Grande Valley, where *quinceañera* parties were not to be missed. I was a *chambelán,* and my date and I were one of fourteen couples in the *quinceañera's* court of honor. The *quinceañera* and her escort made the fifteenth pair—one couple for every year.

Unknown to many Anglos, *quinceañera* parties are the coming-out balls of Mexico and Spanish-speaking Texas, seemingly composed of equal parts wedding, debutante party, and bat mitzvah. The demure fifteen-year-old honoree wears a gown and a veil like a bride, family and friends throw a big bash, and the festivities commence with mass at the Catholic church. A *quinceañera* party signals a girl's coming of age.

Two years after the party, doing my social duty, I traveled to Brownsville for my second go-round. That affair, like the first, was *muy mexicano,* but since Brownsville was a bigger town, the party was bigger and showier. Lines of *damas* and *chambelanes* formed, with the *quinceañera* and her escort leading them. The band struck up some pomp-and-circum-stance march, and we all promenaded around El Jardín hotel ballroom. The room was decked out in crepe paper and bouquets of flowers, and a special spotlight shone on the *quinceañera*. After the promenade she danced with her father as everyone else watched. Then the lights dimmed and the dance opened for the rest of us.

On the drive back home to Mercedes, my father explained that the *quinceañera* parties were a Mexican export. They were held in parts of South America too, he said, and he thought that they must have originated in Spain. In the Valley, though, only those families he called "very mexicanos" held *quinceañera* parties, referring to Mexicans who had been in this country one, perhaps two, generations but who still clung to old Mexican traditions.

Today *quinceañera* parties are major undertakings that begin with a morning mass, followed by a formal reception, a sit-down dinner, and a dance. Instead of just a trio, two bands may play, each with a contract for the number and type of songs to be performed. And instead of donning a homemade white dress, the honoree wears a formal white gown that is as elaborate as the family can afford. As many as one thousand guests may attend, and in the Valley the newspapers report all the fashion details and list the out-of-town guests.

The increase in expenses has made the role of the sponsors—the *padrinos* and the *madrinas*—much more important. Rather than the parents bearing all the cost, the *quinceañera* party has become more of a collaborative effort. And it had to be. Considering that many Valley families earn $8,000 to $10,000 annually, the *padrino-madrina* collective is imperative for a party that can cost as much as $5,000. There are *padrinos* and *madrinas* for just about everything: The dress, hat, gloves, ring, shoes, veil, cake, cake knife, and bouquets, plus the bands, photographers, church services, and myriad other functions. True, this is a once-in-a-lifetime affair, but if there are three girls in the family, what then?

Some businesses and caterers specialize in *quinceañera* parties, and loans may be arranged to pay for them. The expense can be traced back to an old custom, *echar la casa por la ventana*—literally "throw the house out the window"— which means to go all out, no stinting on food or drink, and if the band tries to quit, pay it double. Hang the expense, and see if the next set of parents can top this.

In my present home of Austin, the Mexican professional community, dispersed though it is, maintains a hold on its South Texas–Valley roots and has added twists to the *quinceañera* parties. The professional community and the family may share a genteel and sedate early breakfast with a parish priest. The weekend party is usually small but posh, and depending on the family's cash flow, an out-of-town trip for the *quinceañera* and some of her friends may be arranged. In Houston and Dallas the celebrations are much the same; many Valley people and many "very mexicanos" live there too. And then there's San Antonio, where all four La Feria department stores carry *quinceañera* dresses. In El Paso many Texans buy the festive dresses in Juaréz, which stocks a cornucopia of *quinceañera* gear. Across the *río* it is no different. After all, Mexico exported the *quinceañera* parties, and just like here, the more money a family has, the more it spends on these events. Social pressure is such that whatever the family income, overspending is the rule, and the practice cuts across social lines.

Just how long has this been going on? I have an elaborate 1979 invitation that includes a 1929 picture of a *quinceañera* (now the grandmother), a 1951 photo of the honoree's mother, and a picture of the 1979 *quinceañera*. It has a family tree and pictures of the honoree at birth, baptism, and First Communion and in various ballet and dancing outfits. It also includes the names of the *chambelanes* and *damas;* the announcement that an invitation is required for admission to the reception, dinner, and dance; and a verse written for the *quinceañera* by a friend of her grandfather.

When will the spending stop? Who knows, and why should it? As we say in the Valley, it gives pleasure to many. And with the dresses looking more and more like bridal gowns, perhaps another future expense may be out of the way.

¿Bailamos? "Want to dance?"

IV
Speakin'
la Voz

HARLEM RIVER KISS

Willie Perdomo

Willie Perdomo is the author of Where the Nickel Costs a Dime. *As a poet and as a performer he captures the speed and tension, excitement and sweetness, of being a Nuyorican—a Puerto Rican New Yorker. He is also the author of a children's book,* Visiting Langston, *illustrated by Bryan Collier, that will be published in 2002.*

I hated going to parties in El Barrio. There were mad reasons why, yo. First because it meant that I had to watch my mother dance to "Sexual Healing" in her black spandex pants. Not for nothing, I love the hell out of Mami and for a big woman she can move, but it's torture to watch her dance with her butt all out, exposing her cellulite prints. Then I had to sit through the snapping sessions afterward. My cousins would say that my mother was so fat that if she had a VCR wrapped around her waist it would look like a beeper. Second because Mami's boyfriend, Juan, would come, talking out of the side of his twitching jaws, wearing that crooked, budget, black Borsalino bowler. I called him Don San Juan de Ponce de León. And third because sometimes the party had a way of turning into a weird voodoo feast. Mami and Titi Monchie weren't brujas in the cut-a-rooster-and-use-his-blood-for-spells sense, but something would happen when they played that music with the heavy African drums. They would clap their hands and suddenly flames would come out of their palms and my youngest cousin Puti would go screaming into the kitchen. But I really hated going to parties in El Barrio because I would always end up watching all my cousins make out in the staircase and all I could think about was when would it be my turn to make out.

There was always a celebration at Titi Monchie's house. My family celebrated sweet sixteens, preschool graduation, high-school graduation, new dog, new car, dead cat, anything. Tonight's party was for my prima, Jenny, who was having a baby. Jenny was one of my cousins who was always making out on top of a pile of leather coats, scarves, and gloves with her boyfriend Benny. But at least she wasn't like my cousin Cachita, who made out with a different guy every party. Jenny was going to be a mother and I would have a primita and there would be more birthdays to go to in El Barrio.

Mami was getting dressed when Juan knocked on the door. I knew it was Juan because he always knocked in clavé time. Juan and my uncle Danny would play congas along to Ray Baretto albums and that was actually a reason I liked going to the parties.

"Chuchi, la puerta, mijo!" Mami was in front of the full-length mirror.

I opened the door and Juan walked in with a smile to match his bowler. "Kiddo, y qué? You ready to go to El Barrio?"

"Yeah, man," I said, not really ready.

He headed straight to the bedroom and kissed Mami. They started talking in that low hum that adults use when they don't want kids to hear. Mami asked him if he threw the coconut high into the air so that all the evil it collected splattered into tiny pieces when it hit the street. Then Juan said something about him needing Newports.

"Kiddo!"

"Chuchi!"

They both yelled.

"Huh?"

"Come here, honey," Ma said. I heard her bra straps snap onto her shoulder.

"What's up, Ma?"

"Go to the Dominicanos and tell them that I said to send a pack of Newports with you; that we are getting ready to go a party."

"You should give me a note like last time."

"Qué note y note? Just tell José that it's for me. I'll call him."

"Ma?" I said feeling like there was a good angle to ask a favor in return.

"Qué, mijo?"

"Can I get that baseball glove that we saw in Paragon when we went to your appointment downtown?"

"The one like Jeter?"

"Yeah. That one."

"Bring me an A+ in math and we can talk about it."

"You know I'm not good in math, Ma."

"Yo nunca fui bueno en matemática también," added Juan.

"Nadies estás hablando contigo, Juan. Por favor. Let's see how bad you want that glove."

That meant that I would have to spend more time figuring out isosceles triangles while all my friends played stickball. She gave me the money and on the way out I could hear Juan telling Mami, "You got a good son, Ma," while Mami was on the phone with José from the Dominicanos down the block.

Mr. Softee's music was turning onto Burnside Avenue when I opened the lobby doors. The stoop was crowded. María from 2F and her sisters were playing double dutch in front of the stoop. Up the block, where the lamppost was brightest, the guys from school were playing skelsies, trying hard to get that killer-diller. I would have rather been in on that game than go to the party, but family was family and you could never let them down.

"Hi, Chuchi." María waved.

"Hey, María."

"What's wrong? You sound sad."

"Nothing. We're going to another one of my aunt's parties tonight."

"You'll have fun," she said, handing over the ropes to her sister Coral.

"Come with me to the store, María."

"C'mon," she said, skipping to catch up to me.

María was my girlfriend for about two days and a lunch period, but then she started going out with some kid from Cypress Avenue who was in the tenth grade. But she still was my friend, and I could always count on her for help with algebra equations. The avenue looked like someone came and put a giant plug into the lamppost and suddenly everything came on: the bodega signs, La Mega, gossip, double-dutch ropes, and barking dogs.

José had the pack of Newports ready when he saw me walking through the door.

"Toma, nene. And I'm going to call Marta to make sure she got those cigarettes."

"C'mon, José. Tú sabes que yo no fumo."

"Yo no sé nada. The other day I saw your buddy, Tato, drinking from a bottle of beer."

"That's Tato, not me."

"All right, have fun tonight. Make sure you dance. Girls like men who like to dance."

I knew he was right because that's how María met that kid from Cypress. He asked her to dance when they met at a party in the community center by Hunts Point.

"You still going with the kid from Cypress?" We started walking back to my building.

"Who, Papo?"

"Yeah."

"He comes around the block sometimes to say hi, but we always stay where my mother can see us. Mami doesn't like him. She thinks he's no good for me."

"Then why you see him if your mother doesn't like him?"

"Because it's my heart. Not my mother's." She rolled her eyes.

"You know where you're going to high school next year?" I asked her.

"Probably Manhattan Center."

"In East Harlem?"

"Yeah."

"Oh, that's where I want to go, too."

"Does that mean you're going to need more help with algebra?"

"You know I am."

"No doubt. You know I'm going to always help my boy, Chuchi. Have fun in El Barrio tonight."

"I'll try. You know Mami got her spandex on tonight."

María laughed and her eyes turned real chinita. She said I wasn't right snapping on my own mother. I told her that I would bring reports on the party to lunch period, Monday.

We rode to the party in Juan's brown and beige station wagon with the chipped panels. The ride to Titi Monchie's building was always cool because we had to ride past the Newport cigarette billboard and watch the Newport man blow perfect smoke rings and tell us the time and weather. It was eighty-three degrees, 9:13 P.M. and the moon was following me when we crossed the bridge.

Titi Monchie's building was a six-story walkup with marble steps and no elevators. You could always tell when we got to her neighborhood because there were Puerto Rican flags hanging off everything and Mami would start to complain about having to walk up the stairs. Frankie, my oldest cousin, was sitting in front of the building when we pulled up. A few weeks ago he got a tattoo across his back like the one DMX had with the name of his dog, BOOMER. Frankie's went from shoulder to shoulder and it said PERDON MADRE MIA with a drawing of Jesus Christ hanging on the cross. But instead of hanging his head down, Jesus was looking right at us, eyes wide open. Frank was what Mami called a títere or a thug. He was only nineteen but had spent twenty-two months in a juvenile jail for stealing a car and selling drugs. But ever since he met his girl Lourdes, he's been tranquillo. He works as a messenger and helps Titi Monchie with groceries, cleaning the house, and anything else she needs. I heard the "-ción" of his "bendición" to Mami as she rolled down the window.

"Que dios te bendiga," Mami replied with a kiss. "What are you doing on the street? You know the people are up to no good out here."

"I was using the pay phone to call Lourdes. I needed my privacy. Juan, y qué?"

"Lo mismo, nene. Lo mismo."

"Chuchi, what's up? You gonna sign up for the Goya All-Stars this summer?"

"Yeah, I'm going to Central Park in two weeks."

"Shortstop?" he asked.

"No doubt."

"Is everyone upstairs?" Mami asked.

"Yeah, the whole family. Tío José, Titi Nancy, and Mami's friends from her job."

That meant that all my cousins were up there and the chances that I could go to the bedroom and overdose on the Play Station in peace were slim. We started the climb to the fifth floor and you could hear a guitar like Yomo Toro's. I hated that jíbaro music, but that's the kind of music that Titi Monchie and Mami listened to when they were kids, so they said we had to hear it too.

"Titi Marta, I'm going to pick Lourdes up with Chuchi," Frankie said like he was asking.

"No, no, no. I don't want him out on the street this late."

"C'mon, Ma, let me go with Frankie," I said.

"Déjalo, honey. He's with his primo. He's safe." This is when I didn't mind Juan's bowler so much—when he had my back.

The door to Titi Monchie's was open and you could see that the party started early. Empty eight-ounce cans of Budweiser were on the window sills. Paper plates soaked with pernil stains were on the dining room table and Oscar De León's bass was ready to get into the opening lines of "Llorarás" where he tells his girl that now it's her turn to cry for him.

"Mmuuaaah!" Titi Monchie gave me a big two-lipped kiss on my right cheek. If she'd had red lipstick on she would have left a print of a perfect kiss. I could always depend on Titi Monchie to be an ally.

"Titi Monchie, I'm going with Frankie to pick up Lourdes."

"Did your mother say it was okay?"

Juan put the bug in her ear. Titi Monchie closed the deal. Mami told me that I had to eat before I left. That wasn't too hard. Titi Monchie's arroz con gandules was the best in El Barrio. So I ate that with some tostones and a pork chop. I washed it down with a cold Coco Rico and I left with Frankie. If missing a Yankee game meant missing the spandex sexual healing ballet then I was ready to miss a whole season.

"Where does Lourdes live, Frankie?" I asked as we ran down the stairs two steps at a time.

"In Wagner about ten blocks away." I was hoping he would say something like Queens, where he had to take a bus and a subway. "And she's bringing her little sister with her so you'll have someone to chill with," he said like I should be happy and grateful. Cool, I thought. Now I had someone to watch the *Twilight Zone* with when the party started heading into that slow Tito Rodríguez phase, and my cousins went to the staircase.

Everybody in El Barrio seemed to know Frankie. All you heard on Second Avenue was "Frankie, my dog, whaddup, son?" "Frankie, my man!" "Yo, Frankie, ta tu bien?" Frankie told me, "This is my hood, Chuchi. You want respect, you give respect. You get love when you give love."

When we got to Wagner Houses, Lourdes was already waiting on a green bench under a greener tree. I had to admit that Lourdes was fine and if she were my girlfriend I probably wouldn't resort to crime either. She looked like a mini version of Jennifer López. Word. Butt and everything.

"What's up, ma." Frankie kissed her on the lips and stuck his tongue in her mouth and then sucked on her lips when he took his tongue back. But it all looked like one action. "Lucy, this is my cousin, Chuchi." Frankie pointed to me like he was introducing the next act at a talent show.

"Hi," I said. My heart started beating like Juan was knocking on it. I felt like I was being set up as a decoy. Like it was going to be awhile before we got back to Titi Monchie's house. Lucy said hi back. So soft that I knew I would remember it in my sleep. Juan once told me that there's a difference between a cute woman and a pretty woman. Cute is loud, he said. Pretty is silent like a lily pond or soft rain. Cute girls tried hard to look pretty using bright lipstick and tight clothes. Pretty girls didn't try hard. They didn't try at all. Lucy's eyes were sleepy and her face had no pimples. All the girls in my class had pimples. She was the kind of color that people paid a lot of money to lay on fancy beaches to get. I wanted to tell her that I was shy and that she might have to do all the talking, but my thumping heart kept getting in my mouth's way.

We started walking in the opposite direction of Titi Monchie's building. I started to remind Frankie that we had to get back but I started to have flashes of bowler hats, fire hands, and spandex pants so I decided to stay shut. Besides, if we got in trouble when we got back, Frankie would've been blamed because he's the oldest and he should have known better. We walked past the last building in the projects, next to the Harlem River. The water was shiny like oil. I could see the bridge we took to get to Titi Monchie's as we walked along the pier. Cars zoomed by and there was another island across the river. It was like being on another planet. Frankie and Lourdes would break into laughter and then kiss. When we stopped to sit down, Lucy and I were about to sit on the same bench with Frankie and Lourdes, but they told us to find our own bench. Oh great, I thought, this was the staircase all over again.

"I knew he was up to something," I told Lucy.

"That's okay. My sister does it to me all the time. We go to the movies and she buys me a large popcorn, a large soda, and a box of Jujus and tells me to sit five rows in front of her."

"Oh, that's messed up."

"Yeah, but it keeps my money stash full."

A garbage barge went by in slow motion.

"I wonder where they're taking all that garbage," Lucy said with her head tilted and eyes almost squinted.

"To a landfill. It's like a big abandoned lot with piles and piles of garbage."

"You mean the Bronx?" she asked with a smirk.

"Oh, no! You got jokes from el bummy barrio?"

"Where do you go to school?" she asked.

"I go to I.S. 90. Next year, I'll be in eighth grade."

Frankie and Lourdes were lost in each other's faces. A jogger ran by shadowboxing to the rhythm of music blasting from his headphones.

"I'm going to Manhattan Center, right over there." She pointed to a brown building with gates on the windows.

That's where María wanted to go. I tried to compare Lucy with María. And Lucy was pretty. María was cute. "I want to get into their art program."

"You like to draw?" I asked.

"Paint, too."

"That's cool. You ever kissed a boy?"

I knew I was coming from left field with the kiss question, but I could feel the glow of the Newport clock as the minutes changed. It came down to curiosity. Asking even if she said no—that and knowing how to dance. I had two left feet when it came to getting my groove on, but I had enough curiosity to kill a litter of kittens nine times over.

"Why would you ask me a question like that?" she asked, offended.

"I don't know. I don't mean no disrespect. You're a pretty girl. You talk soft. You like to draw. Juan always says there's a difference between a pretty girl and a cute girl and you're a pretty girl because you don't try hard so I figure you kissed a boy before."

"Who's Juan?"

"He's like my stepfather. When we go to the party he'll be the guy with a funny hat on. Guys must ask you to kiss all the time, right?"

A boat named *Princess Queen* cruised by. There were people dancing in the gold light of the windows.

"They do ask me but then they say they also want to have sex and that's when I say no. So I never kissed a boy because all they want to do is have sex."

I thought about my prima Jenny. For a minute it got so quiet that I heard Frankie ask Lourdes, "You think she likes him?" And Lourdes said, "Yeah, your little cousin seems like he's smart. At least they're talking and he ain't trying to get up all in her."

The bridge was wearing a necklace of lightbulbs. "I like

the way you can see the reflection of the bridge on the river. Do you think you could draw something like that?"

"Yeah, I think so. Why did you ask me about kissing?"

"Because I get tired of coming to these parties and watching my cousins make out in the hallway staircase."

"That's a stupid reason."

There were less cars zooming by. I imagined Mami asking Titi Monchie why we were taking so long to get back. There was a man leaning on a rail with his fishing pole next to him. I wondered what he was trying to catch and if he ever were in my position. And if he was—is that why he was fishing by himself.

"You want to kiss because everyone else is kissing. You should want to kiss someone because you like them, you can talk to them, and you can trust them."

"Chuchi, you ready to go?" Frankie yelled.

I grabbed Lucy's hand and locked her fingers with mine the way Juan holds Mami's hands when they walk down the street. I was surprised when she didn't stop me. This was like dancing without music. Salsa kissing. You lead, she follows. Just don't get too wild and don't try anything too fancy. I looked at her face. It was like a bronze mask dipped in moonlight. A perfect smoke ring came floating over the top of the bridge. I went to kiss her and she stopped me.

"Can I trust you?" she asked.

"Yes, you can trust me."

"Then I want you to meet me at the library after school on Monday and if you're not there, I don't ever want to see you again."

"Okay." I did want to see her again. I couldn't believe that all I had to do was show up at the library. I would even check a book out. Trust. Mami always said that it was important to trust. Friend, girlfriend, whatever, but if there was no trust that was like leaving sofrito out of the arroz con gandules. The love would be sin sabor. I put my other hand softly on the side of her face, by her ear just like the guys did in those black-and-white movies that Mami liked to watch. I put my lips on hers and pulled softly. So my lips looked like they were kissing even if I wasn't doing it right. It was numb at first until I felt the air come between us when I let go. She smiled and kissed me back the same way. I thought my first kiss was going to be in the staircase and I was kind of glad that it wasn't.

"Remember, after school. Your cousin has my sister's phone number so we can talk about drawing and garbage barges." She had dimples when she smiled. I would think of them after her voice.

"You gonna be my girl?"

"I'm going to be your friend first. Then I'll see if you deserve to be my boyfriend."

Frankie walked up to me and said, "Let me find out you Romey Rome, the mack daddy from Cincinnati." Lourdes was laughing and she imitated Lucy's voice, "Ooooh, I'm gonna tell Mom and Pop."

We strolled across a walk bridge and cut through the park, holding hands looking like a smaller copy of Frankie and Lourdes. People were jumping over the gates and sneaking into the public swimming pool in Jefferson Park. Radios were blasting from cars that were parked nearby. It was hard not to think of what was going to happen the next day or what she would look like when we met at the library. I wanted the weekend to be over as soon as we got to the party. I felt like my heart had grown an inch stronger after it got rid of the nervousness. They came to the party and ate some arroz con gandules. Of course, Titi Monchie gave Lourdes a whole shopping bag of food to take home. After Lucy left the party with Lourdes, all my cousins, except me and Frankie, went to the hallway. The adults slow danced, bodies close to each other, while Tito Rodríguez sang them love songs. Frankie was sleeping and I understood why he wanted to stay out of trouble. Lourdes was special and he wanted to keep her. I kept hearing him say, "You get love when you give love." I looked out the window until it was time to go home. It seemed like the plug that had turned on my block was pulled from the socket. A crosstown bus drove by with one passenger sitting in the back. I thought about Lucy waiting for me at the library. I thought about lunchtime on Monday, and how I was going to tell María that I learned how to dance by the river.

Mi Problema

Michele Serros

Michele Serros is known for being a performer. She was born and raised in Oxnard, California. In her shows and stories she explores the tensions that a Chicana woman feels as she tries to balance the culture she gets at home and her experiences outside. In particular, this poem is about the rejection Mexican Americans face because of their poor Spanish-language skills.

My sincerity isn't good enough.
Eyebrows raise
when I request:
"Hable más despacio, por favor."
My skin is brown
just like theirs,
but now I'm unworthy of the color
'cause I don't speak Spanish
the way I should.
Then they laugh **and** talk about
mi problema
in the language I stumble over.

A white person gets encouragement,
praise,
for weak attempts at a second language.
"Maybe he wants to be brown
like us"
and that is good.

My earnest attempts
make me look bad,

dumb.
"Perhaps she wanted to be white
like THEM"
and that is bad.

I keep my flash cards hidden
a practice cassette tape
not labeled
'cause I'm ashamed.
I "should know better"
They tell me
"Spanish is in your blood."

I search for S.S.L. classes
(Spanish as a Second Language)
in college catalogs
and practice with my grandma,
who gives me patience,
permission to learn.

And then one day,
I'll be a perfected "r" rolling
tilde using Spanish speaker.
A true Mexican at last!

MY PROBLEMA
Translated by Melquíades Sánchez

Mi sinceridad no es suficientemente buena.
Se fruncen los ceños
cuando anuncio:
"Hable más despacio, por favor."

Michele Serros

Mi piel es morena
como la de ellos,
pero yo no soy digna del color.
porque no hablo español
como debiera.
Entonces se ríen y murmuran
acerca de mi problema.

A un anglo lo alientan,
le aplauden,
sus precarias intentonas ante una segunda lengua.
"A lo mejor quiere ser moreno
como nosotros"
y eso 'tá bien.

Mis propios esfuerzos
me hacen quedar mal,
como tonta.
"A lo mejor ella quiere ser anglo
como ELLOS"
y eso 'tá mal.

Escondo mis notas de estudio
un cassette con que practico
sin título
porque me avergüenzo.
"Debieras hablar mejor"
me dicen
"el español 'tá en tu sangre."

Busco clases de lengua
(el español como segundo idioma)
en catálogos académicos

y practico
con mi abuela,
que me dá paciencia,
permiso pa' aprender.

Y luego, un día,
por fin barreré la "r" correctamente
pronunciaré como se debe la tilde de "español."
Por fin seré requete mexicana.

La Vida Loca

Luis J. Rodríguez

Luis J. Rodríguez is a former gang member who is now a poet and publisher. As a teenager living a life of street violence, he was lucky to survive. When his own son joined a gang, Rodríguez decided to write a book for him, in the form of a long personal letter. It is called Always Running: La Vida Loca, Gang Days in L.A. *By writing it, Rodríguez dreamed of breaking the cycle of gang violence that devastated his family. The following segment is from the preface. The truths he tells come from hard experience.*

> We have the right to lie, but not about the heart of the matter.
>
> —Antonin Artaud

Late winter Chicago, early 1991: The once-white snow which fell in December had turned into a dark scum, mixed with ice-melting salt, car oil, and decay. Icicles hung from rooftops and windowsills like the whiskers of old men.

For months, the bone-chilling "hawk" swooped down and forced everyone in the family to squeeze into a one-and-a-half-bedroom apartment in a gray-stone, three-flat building in the Humboldt Park neighborhood.

Inside tensions built up like fever as we crammed around the TV set or kitchen table, the crowding made more intolerable because of heaps of paper, opened file drawers, and shelves packed with books that garnered every section of empty space (a sort of writer's torture chamber). The family included my third wife Trini; our child, Rubén Joaquín, born in 1988; and my 15-year-old son Ramiro (a 13-year-old daughter Andrea, lived with her mother in East Los Angeles).

We hardly ventured outside. Few things were worth heaving on the layers of clothing and the coats, boots, and gloves required to step out the door.

Ramiro had been placed on punishment, but not for an act of disobedience or the usual outburst of teenage anxiety. Ramiro had been on a rapidly declining roller coaster ride into the world of street-gang America, not unexpected for this neighborhood, once designated as one of the 10 poorest in the country and also known as one of the most gang-infested.

Humboldt Park is a predominantly Puerto Rican community with growing numbers of Mexican immigrants and uprooted blacks and sprinklings of Ukrainians and Poles from previous generations. But along with the greater West Town area, it was considered a "changing neighborhood," dotted here and there with rehabs, signs of gentrification, and for many of us, imminent displacement.

Weeks before, Ramiro had received a 10-day suspension from Roberto Clemente High School, a beleaguered school with a good number of caring personnel, but one which, unfortunately, was an epicenter of gang activity. The suspension came after a school fight which involved a war between "Insanes" and "Maniacs," two factions of the "Folks." ("Folks" are those gangs allied with the Spanish Cobras and Gangster Disciples; the "People" are gangs tied to the Latin Kings and Vice Lords, symbolic of the complicated structures most inner-city gangs had come to establish.) There was also an "S.O.S."—a "smash-on-sight"—contract issued on Ramiro. As a result, I took him out of Clemente and enrolled him in another school. He lasted less than two weeks before school officials there kicked him out. By then I had also had to pick him up from local jails following other fighting incidents— and once from a hospital, where I watched a doctor put 11 stitches above his eye.

Following me, Ramiro was a second-generation gang

member. My involvement was in the late 1960s and early 1970s in Los Angeles, the so-called gang capital of the country. My teen years were ones of drugs, shooting and beating, and arrests. I was around when South Central Los Angeles gave birth to the Crips and Bloods. By the time I turned 18 years old, 25 of my friends had been killed by rival gangs, police, drugs, car crashes, and suicides.

If I had barely survived all this—to emerge eventually as a journalist, publisher, critic, and poet—it appeared unlikely my own son would make it. I had to cut his blood line to the street early, before it became too late. I had to begin the long, intense struggle to save his life from the gathering storm of street violence sweeping the country—some 20 years after I sneaked out of my 'hood in the dark of night, hid out in an L.A. housing project, and removed myself from the death-fires of *La Vida Loca.*

La Vida Loca or "The Crazy Life" is what we called the barrio gang experience. This lifestyle originated with the Mexican *Pachuco* gangs of the 1930s and 1940s, and was later recreated with the *Cholos.* It became the main model and influence for outlaw bikers of the 1950s and 1960s, the L.A. punk/rock scene in the 1970s and 1980s, and the Crips and Bloods of the 1990s . . .

One evening that winter, after Ramiro had come in late following weeks of trouble at school, I gave an ultimatum. Yelling burst back and forth between the walls of our Humboldt Park flat. Two-year-old Rubén, confused and afraid, hugged my leg as the shouting erupted. In moments, Ramiro ran out of the house, entering the cold Chicago night without a jacket. I went after him, although by my mid-thirties, I had gained enough weight to slow me down considerably. Still, I sprinted down the gangway, which led to a debris-strewn alley, filled with furniture parts and overturned trash cans. I saw Ramiro's fleeing figure, his breath rising above him in quickly dissipating clouds.

I followed him toward Augusta Boulevard, the main drag of the neighborhood. People yelled out the windows and doorways: *"¿Qué pasa, hombre?"* Others offered information on Ramiro's direction. A father or mother chasing some child down the street is not an unfamiliar sight around here.

A city like Chicago has so many places in which to hide. The gray and brown brick buildings seem to suck people in. Ramiro would make a turn and then vanish, only to pop up again. Appearing and disappearing. He flew over brick walls, scurried down another alley, then veered into a building that swallowed him up and spit him out the other side.

I kept after Ramiro until, unexpectedly, I found him hiding in some bushes. He stepped out, unaware I was on the side of him.

"Ramiro . . . come home," I gently implored, knowing if I pounced on him there would be little hope he'd come back. He sped off again.

"Leave me alone!" he yelled.

As I watched him escape, it was like looking back into a distant time, back to my own youth, when I ran and ran, when I jumped over fences, fleeing *vatos locos,* the police, or my own shadow in some drug-induced hysteria.

I saw Ramiro run off and then saw *my* boy entering the mouth of darkness, my breath cutting the frigid flesh of night; it was my voice cracking open the winter sky . . .

After Ramiro ran away, he failed to return home for another two weeks. I was so angry at him for leaving, I bought locks to keep him out. I kept a vigil at home to catch him around should he sneak in to eat. But then I remembered what I had been through. I recalled how many institutions and people had failed my son—and now he was expected to rise above all this! Soon I spent every night he was gone driving around the streets, talking to the "boys" in their street-corner domains, making daily calls to the police. I placed handwritten notes in the basement, which said it was okay for him to come back. I left food for him to get to. Suddenly every teenage Latino male looked like Ramiro.

With the help of some of his friends, I finally found Ramiro in a rundown barrio hovel and convinced him to come home. He agreed to obtain help in getting through some deep emotional and psychological problems—stemming in large part from an unstable childhood, including abuse he sustained as a kid from his stepfathers, one who was an alcoholic and another who regularly beat him. And I could not remove myself from being struck by the hammerhead of responsibility. A key factor was my relative lack of involvement in Ramiro's life as I became increasingly active in politics and writing . . .

Things between us, for now, are being dealt with day by day. Although Ramiro has gained a much more viable perspective on his place in the world, there are choices he has to make "not just once, but every time they come up."

With all the support we tried to muster in the early nineties, Ramiro didn't quite survive the gang's grip on his mind and life. In 1997, he was arrested for three counts of attempted murder and faced 40 years to life—he was 21 years old. But we never abandoned him. The family and community rallied around Ramiro, including with letters of support, so that he wouldn't be sentenced to life.

The judge, after about two and a half years of struggle, ended up sentencing Ramiro to 28 years. That's a long time. It was a moment of madness that pulled Ramiro into this situation. But he is still a much loved and much valued human being. Presently, he's doing all he can to make the most of his time, to finally be released and give proper restitution to his family and community.

We'll be with him every step of the way.

Sugarcane

Achy Obejas

A reporter, novelist, and activist, Achy Obejas was born in Havana and came to the United States in 1963, at the age of six. The characters in her books, many of them independent women fighting for their right to be heard in society, confront the machismo of Hispanic society and explore the differences between living the traditional life in Cuba and getting an education in the United States. While Ricardo Pau-Llosa in "Frutas" gets a sense of how far he is from Cuba through the tropical fruits he can still find in America, Obejas tries to imagine Cuba from faraway Chicago.

can't cut
cut the cane
azuca' in chicago
dig it down to the
roots sprouting spray paint on the
walls on the hard cold
stone of the great gritty city
slums in chicago
with the mansions in the hole
in the head of
the old rich left behind
from other times lopsided
gangster walls overgrown taken
over by the dark
and poor overgrown with no
sugarcane but you
can't can't cut

cut the water
bro'
from the flow and
you can't can't cut
cut the blood
lines from this island
train one by one throwing off
the chains siguaraya
no no
no se pue'e cortar
pan con ajo quisqueya
cuba y borinquen no
se pue'en parar

I saw it
saw black a-frica
down in the city
walking in chicago y
la cuba cuba
gritando en el solar
I saw it
saw quisqueya
brown
uptown in the city
cryin' in chicago
y borinquen
bro'
sin un
chavo igual but
you can't can't cut
cut the water
bro'
from the flow and
you can't can't cut

cut the blood
lines from this island
train one by one throwing off
the chains siguaraya
no no
no se pue'e cortar
pan con ajo quisqueya
cuba y borinquen no
se pue'en parar

¡azuca'!

CAÑA DE AZÚCAR
Translated by the author and Argelia Fernández

no se pue' cortar
cortar la caña
azúca' en chicago
sacarla de raíz
pa' pintar dolor en
las piedras blanca fría
de la gran ciudad descarná'
solares en chicago
mansiones en el agujero
derrumbándose
en la memoria de los viejos millonarios
las paredes pandilleras cayéndose
tomadas por malezas
ahora a cargo de negros y pobres
no hay caña aquí
no brother no
no cortes el agua

bro'
la corriente
no puedes no se pue'e cortar
cortar los hilos de sangre
de este cuerpo isleño
cada isla soltando las cadenas
no no
no se pue'e cortar
pan con ajo quisqueya
cuba y borinquen no
se pue'en parar

la ví
ví a Africa negra
en la ciudad
caminando por chicago y
la cuba cuba
gritando en el solar
la ví
ví a quisqueya
brown
en el norte
llorando en chicago
y borinquen
bro'
sin un
chavo igual pero
no hay caña aquí
no brother no
no cortes el agua
bro'
la corriente
no puedes no se pue'e cortar
cortar los hilos de sangre

de este cuerpo isleño
cada isla soltando las cadenas
no no
no se pue'e cortar
pan con ajo quisqueya
cuba y borinquen no
se pue'en parar

¡azuca'!

THE LEMON STORY

Alberto Alvaro Ríos

Alberto Alvaro Ríos is a poet and teacher from Nogales, Arizona. His upbringing in the U.S.-Mexican border town is powerfully conveyed in the memoir Capirotada. *The title refers to Mexican bread pudding, made of prunes, peanuts, white bread, raisins, milk, quesadilla cheese, butter, cinnamon, cloves, sugar—"all this," says Ríos, "and things people will not tell you." His evocative book is also a mix of family members, friends, and neighbors.*

When I was about four, or maybe five, my parents bought a new house in what would later become a small suburb of Nogales, Arizona, on the border of Mexico, some four miles outside town. My father was born in Mexico, on the border of Guatemala, and my mother was born in England. From the very start I had many languages.

As we kept driving out to watch the house being built, my mother got to make a number of choices regarding details, among which was the color of various rooms.

My mother, when asked what color she wanted the kitchen, said to the workers, who were all Mexican and who spoke very little English, *limón*. She said it both because she wanted the kitchen to be yellow and because she wanted to start learning Spanish. The workers nodded yes. But when she came back the next day, the kitchen was painted bright green, like a small jungle. Mexican *limones,* my mother found out, are small and green, that color exactly, no mistake.

So that's the color that wall stayed for the next fourteen years, until I left home for college. She said it was a reminder to us all that there was a great deal to learn in the world. You might laugh at first, but after fourteen years you start to think about it.

'TWAS THE NIGHT

María Eugenia Morales

María Eugenia Morales, a native of San Antonio, where she was born in 1971, shows that in the United States today, as we mix and match cultures and languages, a very North American Christmas has a whole new accent.

'Twas the night before Christmas and all through the casa
Not a creature was stirring, caramba! Qué pasa?
Los niños were tucked away in their camas
Some in vestidos and some in pijamas.
While Mamá worked in her little cocina,
El viejo was down at the corner cantina.
The stockings were hanging with mucho cuidado,
In hopes that Saint Nicholas would feel obligado
To bring all the children both buenos and malos
A nice bunch of dulces and other regalos.
Outside in the yard, there arose such a grito
That I jumped to my feet like a frightened cabrito.
I ran to the window and looked afuera,
And who in the world do you think that it era?
Saint Nick in a sleigh and a big red sombrero
Came dashing along like a crazy bombero!
And pulling his sleigh, instead of venados,
Were eight little burros approaching volados.
I watched as they came and this quaint little hombre
Was shouting and whistling and calling by nombre:
"Ay Chato! Ay Pepe! Ay Cuca! Ay Beto!
Ay Pancho! Ay Chopo! Maruca y Nieto!"
Then standing erect with his hand on his pecho,
He flew to the top of our very own techo!

With his round little belly like a bowl of jalea,
He struggled to squeeze down our old chimenea,
Then huffing and puffing, at last in our sala,
With soot smeared all over his red suit de gala;
He filled the stockings with lovely regalos,
For none of the niños had been very malos.
Then chuckling along, seeming very contento,
He turned like a flash and was gone like el viento.
And I heard him exclaim and this is verdad,
"Merry Christmas to all, Feliz Navidad!"

DEAR ROSITA

Nash Candelaria

Born in Los Angeles in 1928, Nash Candelaria is descended from settlers who helped found Albuquerque, New Mexico, in 1706. He lives in Santa Fe. "Dear Rosita" is told through letters between a father and daughter. She is the first one in the family to go to college and is rapidly loosening ties to the culture and questioning the values she grew up with.

Dear Rose,

See, I remember to call you Rose instead of Rosita. Now that you left New Mexico to go to that Eastern university I guess you need a name that fits. So I'll write Rose from now on. Tho your old papá will always think of you as his Rosita.

Mamá says hi. Says now she wished she had gone to school so she could write to you. Except times were hard then. She had to go to work almost as soon as she learned to walk. But she's glad times are better now and *you* can go. The first one in the family to go to college. She's very proud of you. With your scholarship and everything. She shake her fist and say, "Show 'em, Rosie. Show 'em what kind of stuff Sandoval women are made of."

Sometimes at night I catch her leaning on the adobe wall staring out the window with tears in her eyes. "Where's Massachusetts?" she says. "Do the pilgrims still live there? And how about the madam on the boat?" she say. "The *Mayflower*. Mrs. González told me about that. That's not very nice."

I tell her not to worry. You're not going on any boat. You're at the university.

Your little brothers and sisters say hello and send you kisses. They say to send them a souvaneer from back East. They ask, "Is your university in one of those tall buildings like on TV? Do the people live in those tall buildings too? Where do they keep the children and the goats? (Hah!) And how can you get any sunshine if you're always indoors and there are no fields?"

The kids have been very good since you've been gone. The corn crop was so big that they worked extra hard this year. Panchito picked more than anybody. Almost as much as a man. And he sold at our stand all by himself when I had to take Mamá to the doctor.

Well, that's all for now. I got to go to the corral and feed the animals.

Love,

Papá

Dear Rose,

We receive your letter. We think it very funny that the woman at the university post office said you had to pay extra to send T-shirts because she didn't think New Mexico was in the United States. At least I think it funny. Mamá got mad. "What kind of dumb university is that where they don't know their states?" she say. "How they are going to teach our daughter anything?"

Panchito's teacher say there is a magazine here called *New Mexico*. The state prints it. Every month there is a page called "One of Our Fifty Is Missing." It tells about other dumb people who don't know where New Mexico is. They think it Old Mexico which is another country.

The kids are crazy for the T-shirts with the university name on the front. Everybody at their school is jealous. Sometimes they play like they go to university like their big sister. It must cost a lot to buy eight T-shirts. I know you have this job in the Affirmative Action office at school. But you say you have to read six hours a day for your homework. So either you can't work too much and earn money. Or you don't sleep enough which is not healthy. Or those smart professors found how to stretch the day to 28 hours. Anyway, there was lots of corn this year. We earned a little extra so I am sending you a money order to help with the T-shirts.

How was your Thanksgiving there in the land of the pilgrims? Around here the Indians don't eat much turkey but corn and chile and frijoles like us. Or cabrito. There is nothing so good as bar-b-q goat. But we roasted some chickens this year. And the corn was so sweet and so tender.

I am so sorry you can't come home for Xmas. It will be the first time ever we won't be all together. We'll hang out your stocking and save it for you when you come home next summer. Santa won't forget his Rose.

Well, time to open the sluice gate to the acequia. It has been dry so we need to fill the ditch with more water from the Río Grande.

Love,
Papá

Dear Rose,
What's all this about I'm not supposed to eat meat? All my life I was too poor to buy much meat. I mean like round steak or roast. Now that things are better and we can afford beef, there's all this worry about your heart. Don't eat meat! You say we suppose to eat fish. But tell me. You grew up here in Los Rafas. You know it's desert. Where you going to get fish in the desert? Sure, we could go up north in the mountains and fish for trout. It's only an hour by car. But who has the time even if your car is running OK? There's too much to do on our little plot of ground.

Not only that. Now I hear that beans are *good* for you. Lots of protein. Very high fiber too. So you can go to the excusado regular. Any fool could have told you that. Then some smart doctor says that chile is good for the blood. Cleans out the fat or something. Another smarty doctor says we need more exercise. More exercise? I bet he never did anything harder than push pills. Just send him down to the country to work the land for a summer. He'll know what exercise is. Who needs to go out and run on purpose? Or sweat and breathe hard on purpose? Man, that's the way we *live*— sweating and breathing hard.

So here I am. Practically an old man who spent his life on the land, one of the working poor. I've had a little luck so I can enjoy my old age, and now what? They tell me: Don't give up chile and beans for steak and potatoes. Continue to work like a dog in the fields. Do all that and you live longer. Maybe not happier but longer. Like the Bible says, if you wait long enough the seasons change and everything comes back to you. Who needs it?

Anyway, I got to go out in the field and sweat again so I can live to a ripe old age.

Love,
Papá

Dear Rose,

That was very interesting what you write us about the Big Bang. When I first mentioned Big Bang your mamá got real mad. "Is that what they teach her at those Godless universities—" she say, "how to talk dirty?"

Then I explain to her that it's not dirty at all. It's just science. These guys with big brains, they sit around figuring how things work. Like how the world began. And the Big Bang was at the beginning of the time when everything exploded and made the earth and stars and everything.

"Explosions?" she say. "Hah! Any fool knows that when things blow up they break apart into a million pieces. So how can that be the beginning of the world with things breaking apart? Those professors been sitting around in their rooms so long that the blood drained to their butts. They gone loco. Like old Señora Armijo who thinks that she flies through the desert when she falls asleep at night. When you don't know the dream from the real thing, you're in big trouble."

Then she looked at me with the look that could scare the devil himself. "And anyway," she say, "what about Adam and Eve? You think they gonna live through an explosion? Explain to me, smart guy. Tell that to the priest the next time you go to confession."

Well, you know your mamá. The best thing is to shut up and give her a couple days to cool off. Anyway, I don't understand this Big Bang thing enough to argue with her. So I went out to the corral and read your letter again.

Mamá had a good point. What about Adam and Eve? And the apple and the snake? It wouldn't take much of a bang for them to be blown to pieces. But even more important, hija. Do you still go to church? I hope you don't let all this science and all this smart talk turn you away from God. Next thing you know you'll be joining the zoo keepers who tell us we came from the monkeys. Although sometimes like with your mamá's older brother, your uncle Luis, I wonder. Anyway, please. Don't turn away from God. Remember to go to mass every Sunday and holy day of obligation. And say your prayers every morning and night. We want you to come back to us the same sweet daughter who left.

I'm gonna go and say a little prayer for you right now. God bless you. And be smart, but not so smart you forget God.

Love,
Papá

Dear Rose,

What's all this about bail? I didn't tell your mamá because I knew it would break her heart. Not only are you the first in the family to go to college, you are the first to need bail.

I don't understand why anybody has to take over the university president's office. Any fool knows that those big shots got the cops on their side. The little guy hasn't got a chance. If the cops aren't enough, they can call out the marines. Or— like Panchito say—they nuke 'em.

Anyway, it didn't make the newspapers here so you don't have to worry about that. Nobody knows but me, and I won't tell even if they cut my tongue off.

I know I'm not an educated man. But there's some things I learn just by living. And one of them is never bite the hand that feed you. I mean I like the scholarships and things. Another is, you can't fight city hall. Which means don't take over the president's office.

Sure. I know that you feel that there aren't enough Chicano and Black and Chinese professors. Everybody like to see some of their own kind make good. Have a professor who understands what you come from and how hard you worked for it. How much you want a chance like everybody else. But Rose, you got to do things the right way.

What you do now, Rose, is make an appointment with the president. Go see him and have a nice talk. Be honest with him. If he is the right kind of guy, he will understand. If he don't understand, do what we did in the fields when a skinflint farmer didn't pay a living wage. The crops, they just come up once a year. You don't pick at the right time—boom! There goes every red cent you planned to harvest. Well, colleges are like that too. Only their crops are students. They're student farmers. And if a farm don't turn out crops, they don't make money. If they don't make money, they get a new farmer or the banks take over the farm. I don't want to sound like no revolutionary, but that's how I see it. It worked in the fields. Maybe it will work in the colleges. It's something you can do without staying arrested. Which means you don't have to pay bail.

Anyway, the goats are making a racket in the corral. They say they go on strike if I don't feed them. Everybody wants something from somebody. That's all for now.

Love,

Papá

Dear Rose,

I been thinking about bail since the last time I wrote. Lots of good people been put in jail. Jesus. That Indian man Gandhi. I don't remember who else, but lots of good people. I don't know if George Washington ever got arrested, but I bet if those red coats had got him they'd have locked him up for life plus a hundred years.

What reminded me was cleaning out the old shed. You didn't know but we going to make a room from it and cut a door into the rest of the house. We need another room to separate the boys and the girls. They getting older, and it's the right thing to have a room for the boys and another for the girls.

Anyway, I found these old newspapers. Some of them go° way back. This was before your time, and I'm sure you don't remember it. But there was that big land problem up north in Tierra Amarilla maybe 20, 25 years ago. The people they got into a—I don't know what you call it. Maybe a war. With the government. About who the land belong to and who can do what to it.

Anyway. There on the front page is this big picture. This paisano with his cow. The cow is staring over the barb wire fence. And the farmer, he got tears in his eyes and he say: "My cow, she arrested." Alongside the cow—her name was

Dolores—was this government chota, shiny badge, holster with a gun and all, holding a rope. The other end was around Dolores's neck.

Seems like Dolores, she's a naughty girl. She go through a broken place in the fence into this field that say "U.S. Government. No Trespassing." But Dolores, she can't read. So this cop, he tie a rope around her neck and arrest her. I wonder if he read her her rights? And the poor old farmer, he has to pay the bail. Or maybe it was a fine. Anyway, I wonder if they really put that cow in a cell? Sounds pretty silly to me. Specially since the fence was broke, and how's a cow supposed to know? Just one of God's dumb creatures.

So I guess you are not in bad company. Jesus. Gandhi. Maybe George Washington. And Dolores the cow. Only don't let it happen again if you can help it. Someday somebody may not have bail.

That's all for now. I promised to take Mamá to church tonight. We say a prayer for you.

Love,

Papá

Dear Rose,

Oh, how sad we all are that you may stay and work back East this summer. It seems so long since we see you. Tina start to cry, and then your mamá. Pretty soon everybody. So it was like a flood in the house. The linoleum in the front room had tear spots all over. We hardly talked. Just worked. At supper we could not look in each other's eyes. Then your next letter came that said you were coming home. Everybody start to smile and laugh again.

Don't worry about the money. If you don't find a job here, we will help you. Money isn't everything. I mean you need enough to get along. But whether you eat beans or steak don't matter as long as you eat. (And I learn from you this year that beans are better.) Money you can always earn. But not seeing your friends, not seeing your family. That's something if you miss, you never get back. Your little brothers and sisters grow so much since you went away. You'd hardly know them. Now Panchito, he say he going to college too. They all so proud of their big sister and want so much to see you.

Your mamá have this fear. She say, "How am I going to talk to her? I never talk to no college person except when I go to the doctor. What am I going to say? What if she's changed? Is she going to be ashamed of her mamá who can't even write her a letter? Oh, I'm so worried."

Worry, worry, worry. She worry you don't come. She worry you *do* come. I just say, "Relax. Just tell her you love her. She the same daughter you used to nurse and change diapers and all that. She still learn a thing or two from you. So don't worry. It'll be fine. Besides. I bet she can't cook like you. Not yet."

But the truth is, I worry a little too. We are so proud of you. And want you not to be ashamed of us poor country folks. You are going up in the world. Only like the old story: Don't get too close to the sun or it melt your wings and down you go.

Look for us at the station when your bus comes in. Panchito nag his sisters and brothers to wash and iron their university T-shirts. That's so you can tell who they are because they grown so much since you gone. They think you be a grown lady like a princess in the movies now that you been in the university one year. They are so excited.

God love you and speed you home safely. We are so excited our hearts will burst. So hurry home. We can hardly wait to see you next week.

With love from all,
Papá

CHILD OF THE AMERICAS

Aurora Levins Morales

Aurora Levins Morales was born in 1954. Her mother, Rosario, was born in 1930 and moved from New York to Puerto Rico after she got married. In Getting Home Alive, a collection of writings compiled in collaboration with her mother, Aurora Levins Morales explores how differently the older and younger generations assimilate to life in the United States. "Child of the Americas" is a statement of the way Levins Morales understands her American identity.

I am a child of the Americas,
a light-skinned mestiza of the Caribbean,
a child of many diaspora, born into this continent at a
    crossroads.

I'm a U.S. Puerto Rican Jew,
a product of the ghettos of New York I have never known.
An immigrant and the daughter and granddaughter of
    immigrants.
I speak English with passion: It's the tool of my con-
    sciousness,
a flashing knife blade of crystal, my tool, my craft.

I am a Caribeña, island grown, Spanish is in my flesh,
ripples from my tongue, lodges in my hips:
the language of garlic and mangoes,
the singing in my poetry, the flying gestures of my hands.
I am of Latinoamérica, rooted in the history of my
    continent:

I speak from that body.

I am not african. Africa is in me, but I cannot return.
I am not taína. Taíno is in me, but there is no way back.
I am not european. Europe lives in me, but I have no
home there.

I am new. History made me. My first language was
spanglish.
I was born at the crossroads
and I am whole.

Hija de las Américas
Translated by Ilan Stavans

Soy hija de las Américas,
una mestiza clara del Caribe,
hija de muchas diásporas, nacida en este continente en la
encrucijada.

Soy una judía puertorriqueña norteamericana,
producto de los ghettos de Nueva York que nunca
conocí.
Una inmigrante y la hija y nieta de inmigrantes.
Hablo inglés con pasión: es la herramienta de mi con-
ciencia,
mi cuchillo de cristal, mi herramienta, mi oficio.

Soy caribeña, isleña, el español está en mi carne,
baila desde mi lengua, se deposita en mis caderas.
La lengua de ajo y mangos,
el cantar de mi poesía, los gestos volantes de mis manos.

Soy de Latinoamérica, enraizada en la historia de mi con-
tinente:
hablo desde ese cuerpo.

No soy africana. Africa está en mí, pero no puedo volver.
No soy taína. Lo taíno está en mí, pero no hay camino de
regreso.
No soy europea. Europa vive en mí, pero allí no tengo
hogar.

Soy nueva. La historia me hizo. Mi primera lengua fue el
espanglish.
Nací en la encrucijada
y soy completa.

Fragmentos/
Fragments

Demetria Martínez

Demetria Martínez was born in 1960 and lives in Tucson, Arizona. She has been a reporter and an activist. Her compassionate poems explore the tension between Spanish and el inglés, between her Mexican background and her life as a citizen of the United States.

Escribo esta cartita en español
y es como conducir sin manos,
es como el sueño de volar,
un sentido de poder, el temor
de caer. Inglés. Mi máscara,
mi espada. En su lugar, este
kimono de palabras, este huipil.
Palabras que dejan que entre viento y
sol. Toco la seda, toco el algodón.
¿Quién es la mujer en el espejo?
Quiero conocerla.

I write this letter in Spanish, and it is like driving without hands, a dream of flight, a feeling of power, a fear of falling. English. My mask, my sword. In its place, this kimono of words, this *huipil*. Words that let in wind and sun. I touch the silk, the cotton. Who is the woman in the mirror? I want to know her.

Cada
palabra
que escribo
en español
es una luna

hole punched in the dark
with a pen

mi cara en
esta luz
mis ojos
mis labios
¿seré yo?

Each
word
I write
in Spanish
is a moon

hole punched in the dark
with a pen

my face
in this light
my eyes
my lips
is it really me?

Sometimes frightened,
I run back to the familiar
streets of English.

I go about my usual business,
making things go my way
at the bank, store, government office,

moving mountains in English
not by faith but by precision,
words aimed between eyes.

In moments of grace,
poetry or prayer,
English uses me.

But most of the time, I use it.
I do not always like what I
have become in this tongue.

Es distinto en español.
Escribo esta carta, paso a paso
por fe, en esta media luz,
algunas veces parando
para pedir direcciones.

Cuando no conozca una palabra
dejo un blank ___ así.
Llevo estos blanks conmigo
como velas hasta que alguien
me ayude con un fósforo.
Y estos blanks.
se transforman
en gotas de luz para guiarme
hasta que pueda dejar
las velas al lado del camino,
una ofrenda, una constelación
de sueños para los que siguen.

It is different in Spanish
I write this letter, step by step,
by faith, in this half-light,
at times stopping
to ask for directions.

And when I don't know a word
I leave a blank ___ like this.
I carry these blanks with me
like candles until someone
stops to help, lights a match.
Emptiness giving way
to light that guides me
so that I can leave the candles
at the side of the road,
an offering, a constellation
of dreams for those who follow.

Hablarte
en esta lengua
es como desnudarme
por la primera vez
ante tus ojos.
Temor, deseo,
sin volver . . .

Speaking to you
in this tongue is like
undressing for the first time
before your eyes.
Fear, desire,
No turning back . . .

—gracias a Teresa Márquez

GLOSSARY

Since the arrival of the Iberian explorers to Florida and the Southwest, *el español* has been a fixture of this land. But as the Hispanic population has grown in size and spread, its interaction with English has become global. The entries in this anthology are a celebration, acknowledgment, and reflection of that interaction. With the exception of Demetria Martínez's "Fragments/*Fragmentos*," Cecilio García-Camarillo's "Talking to the Río Grande," and María Eugenia Morales's "'Twas the Night," which are deliberately drafted in a robust verbal give-and-take beyond translation, the *corridos* and poems appear in bilingual format. The terms in this glossary, then, are those that cannot be figured out in context, for example, proper names, historical sites, or terms in Spanish that are completely unlike the parallel words in English. Assuming that my readers live in a world where languages and cultures are already mixed, I have avoided defining cognates and well-known cultural terms such as *amigo* and *enchilada*. That kind of false completeness would actually make the glossary less useful to readers, who would be likely to find it silly.

Acequia: Irrigation ditch.
Alvaro Obregón: Mexican president, 1920–24. He was
    elected again in 1928 but assassinated that same year.
Ándale, ándale: Come on, come on!
Así nomás: Just like that!
Benditos: Good God!
Borinquén: Puerto Rico.
Caimito: A tropical fruit.
Carola: Christmas carol.
Chambelán: Male teenage member of the *quinceañera*
    court.

Chingadera: Pain in the neck.

Colación: Candy assortment.

Conga: A large drum; a Cuban carnival dance.

Coyote: U.S.-Mexican border trafficker.

Cuánta cebolla: So much onion!?

Dale, dale: Hurry up, hurry up!

Damas: Ladies.

Dámaso Pérez Prado: Mambo-rhythm musician.

Deportee: Illegal worker who is returned home.

Distrito Federal: Mexico City.

El otro lado: The other side.

Factoría: Factory.

Feelin: Spanglish for feeling.

Fidel Castro: Long-standing Marxist leader from Cuba, who reached power in the 1958–59 armed revolution.

Gusano: Exiled Cuban in Miami.

Hable más despacio: Speak slowly.

Híjole: Wow!

Jodido: Miserable.

Joto: Homosexual.

Huipil: Typical woman's tunic from the Yucatán peninsula.

La voz: The voice.

Limón: Lime.

Locotes: The crazy ones.

Luis Echeverría Alvarez: Mexican president, 1970–76.

Mamey: Tropical fruit.

'Mana: Mexican slang for female friend.

Maña: Strategy.

Mariyandá: A Brazilian fruit.

Me quemo: I'm getting burned.

Miedoso: Scaredy-cat.

Mongo: Cuban slang for "stupid."

Niñera: Baby-sitter.

Pa'late: Moving forward.

Pa'trás: Moving backward.

Papiamiento: Street language.

Por favor: Please!

Posada: Christmas festivity from Mexico.

Pues: That is; in other words.

Qué peste: How troublesome!

Rápido, rápido: Quick, quick!

Reata: Cord.

Rootas: Spanglish for roots.

Tilde: Mark (~) put on the letter *n* in Spanish.

Vaquero: Cowboy.

Vas muy despacio: You're too slow.

Vatos locos: Crazed punks.

Verga: Valor. Also used to describe the male sexual organ.

Vivas: Hurray!

Wáchale: Look out! See epigraph at the beginning of Introduction.

Ya anda repelando el mayordomo: The boss is complaining already!

Ya no aguanto: I can't bear it anymore!

Ya párale: Stop it!

Further Readings

I have selected books by authors included in this volume that, for some reason, may be of special interest to younger readers. Few were written with that audience in mind, but in each case I have indicated why, for example, the topic, language, or voice speaks across generations. Needless to say, this is not meant to be a complete bibliography; instead, it is a highly personal and selective guided tour for readers to use in their own explorations.

There are very few anthologies of Latino literature meant for middle schoolers. Worthy of notice are *Growing Up Latino: Memoirs and Stories,* edited by Harold Augenbraum and Ilan Stavans (Houghton Mifflin, 1993), which offers a smorgasbord of Latino voices, old and new; and *Cool Salsa,* edited by Lori Carlson (Holt, 1995), poetry in English and Spanish exclusively targeted for young readers. Several relevant anthologies are meant for the general market. Some of them, with partial content suitable for this readership, are *Iguana Dreams: New Latino Fiction,* edited by Delia Poey and Virgil Suárez (HarperCollins, 1992); *Paper Dance: 55 Latino Poets,* edited by Victor Hernández Cruz, Leroy V. Quintana, and Virgil Suárez (Persea, 1995); *New World: Young Latino Writers,* edited by Ilan Stavans (Delta, 1997); *The Latino Reader: From 1542 to the Present,* edited by Harold Augenbraum and Margarite Fernández Olmos (Houghton Mifflin, 1997); *Floricanto Sí! A Collection of Latina Poetry,* edited by Bryce Milligan, Mary Guerrero Milligan, and Angela De Hoyos (Penguin, 1998); and *Latino Writers in the U.S.* (Nextext, McDougal Littell, 2001).

Behar, Ruth. *Translated Woman: Crossing the Border with Esperanza's Story.* Boston: Beacon Press, 1993. The chronicle of a passionate relationship between an anthropologist and a lower-class Mexican woman. The language used might be too elevated for teenagers.

Candelaria, Nash. *The Day the Cisco Kid Shot John Wayne*. Tempe, AZ: Bilingual Press/Editorial Bilingüe, 1988. Witty, sharp tales about coming of age as a Chicano in the Southwest. Also appropriate is *Uncivil Rights and Other Stories* (Bilingual Press, 1998), consisting of accessible narratives where characters come to terms with their ancestry and place in the world.

Colón, Jesús. *A Puerto Rican in New York and Other Sketches*. New York: International Publishers, 1982. Sharp, distinctive vignettes delivered in simple prose, about Puerto Rican life in New York in the mid-twentieth century.

Espada, Martín. *City of Coughing and Dead Radiators*. New York: W. W. Norton, 1993. Compassionate poems with a strong political tone. The direct language and urgency of the message should appeal to young readers.

García-Camarillo, Cecilio. *Selected Poetry of Cecilio García-Camarillo*. Introduction by Enrique R. Lamadrid. Houston, TX: Arte Publico Press, 2000. A generous selection of poems for a wide range of audiences, originally published in chapbooks—self-made, inexpensive booklets meant for a small readership.

González, Jovita. *The Woman Who Lost Her Soul and Other Stories*. Edited, with an introduction, by Sergio Reyna. Houston, TX: Arte Publico Press, 2000. These stories are based on border myths that have animals as characters, explore popular customs and religious rites, and often involve ghosts and demons. Like much folklore, they are easy reads, yet have a great deal to say.

Hinojosa-Smith, Rolando. *Klail City*. Houston, TX: Arte Publico Press, 1987. An enduring saga about a fictional town in the Río Grande Valley. Other installments include *Rites and Witnesses* (Arte Publico Press, 1982), *Partners in Crime* (Arte Publico Press, 1985), *Dear Rafe* (Arte Publico Press, 1985), *Becky and Her Friends* (Arte Publico Press, 1990), and *The Useless Servants* (Arte Publico Press, 1993). Several of the volumes will appeal to young readers.

Hospital, Carolina, ed. *Cuban American Writers: Los Atrevidos*. Princeton, NJ: Ediciones Ellas/Linden Lane Press in association with Co/Works, Inc., 1988. Groundbreaking anthology that includes numerous pieces for middle schoolers. In Spanish *los atrevidos* means "the daring ones." The entries of this volume explore various aspects of Cuban life in the United States, including tension between the old and young generations in their relationship with the homeland.

Levins Morales, Aurora, with Rosario Morales. *Getting Home Alive.* Ithaca, NY: Firebrand Books, 1986. A readable collection of mother-daughter collaborations that addresses issues of assimilation. Several portions of it are appropriate for young readers.

Martí, José. *The America of José Martí.* Translated by Juan de Onís. Introduction by Federico de Onís. New York: Noonday Press, 1953. A valuable selection of the poet's work, with many poems and anecdotes for young readers.

Martínez, Demetria. *Mother Tongue.* New York: One World, 1996. Engaging novel about immigrant life. Some of the issues addressed might be too sophisticated for teenagers.

Martínez, Dionisio D. *Climbing Back.* New York: W. W. Norton, 2001. Lyrical, evocative collection about nostalgia and endurance among Cuban exiles. The crisp language should make portions attractive to teenagers.

Mora, Pat. *My Own True Name: New and Selected Poems for Young Adults, 1984–1999.* Mora writes directly for younger readers, so many of her works could be listed here. Designed for younger audiences are *Tomás and the Library Lady* (Knopf, 1997) and *This Big Sky* (Knopf, Scholastic, 1998).

Obejas, Achy. *We Came All the Way from Cuba So You Could Dress Like This?* Pittsburgh, PA: Cleis Press, 1994. Stories about assimilation by Cubans into mainstream American culture, from the viewpoint of women. Also of note is *Days of Awe* (Ballantine, 2001), a novel about life in Cuba and the United States.

Ortiz Cofer, Judith. *Silent Dancing: A Partial Remembrance of a Puerto Rican Childhood.* Houston, TX: Arte Publico Press, 1991. Accessible memoir about a Puerto Rican girl in Patterson, New Jersey. Also for young readers is *An Island Like You* (Chronicle, 1995) and *The Year of Our Revolution* (Arte Publico Press, 1998), a collection of prose and poetry.

Palés Matos, Luis. *Selected Poems/Poesía selecta.* Translated, with an introduction, by Julio Marzán. Houston, TX: Arte Publico Press, 2000. A useful anthology of the poet's robust Afro-Caribbean lyrics, with mesmerizing portions accessible to young readers.

Pau-Llosa, Ricardo. *Bread of the Imagined.* Tempe, AZ: Bilingual Press/Editorial Bilingüe, 1992. Vivid collection, where the poet explores time and space through language. Several poems are suitable for young readers.

Perdomo, Willie. *Where a Nickel Costs a Dime.* New York: W. W. Norton, 1996. Perdomo's lively voice sprinkled with street talk should appeal to readers, especially teenagers, who enjoy rap.

Ríos, Alberto Alvaro. *Capirotada: A Nogales Memoir.* Albuquerque: University of New Mexico Press, 1999. Potent autobiography, with keen prose, about family life on the U.S.-Mexican border. Also valuable for middle schoolers are portions in *Pig Cookies and Other Stories* (Chronicle, 1995) and *The Iguana Killer: Twelve Stories of the Heart* (University of New Mexico Press, 1998).

Rodríguez, Luis J. *Always Running: La Vida Loca, Gang Days in L.A.* Willimantic, CT: Curbstone Press, 1993. Memorable chronicle of life as a gang member and a father-son relationship. Includes violent segments and strong language.

Sánchez, Rosaura. *He Walked In and Sat Down, and Other Stories.* Translated by Beatrice Pita. Albuquerque: University of New Mexico Press, 2000. The accessibility of some of the stories will be embraced by young readers.

Serros, Michele. *Chicana Falsa, and Other Stories of Death, Identity, and Oxnard.* New York: Riverhead Books, 1998. Written with humor and zest, these pieces about Chicanas in and out of the mainstream will speak to those ready to laugh and be serious at the same time. Also valuable is *How to Be a Chicana Role Model* (Riverhead, 2000).

Soto, Gary. *Baseball in April and Other Stories.* San Diego: Harcourt Brace Jovanovich, 1990. Popular collection of growing-up tales from the viewpoint of a beloved Chicano author for children and young readers. Also of note among Soto's numerous titles is *Buried Onions* (HarperCollins, 1999), a narrative in which a nineteen-year-old drops out of college and struggles to find a place for himself as a Mexican American living in a violence-infested neighborhood of Fresno, California.

Stavans, Ilan. *On Borrowed Words.* New York: Viking, 2001. An autobiographical account of childhood as a Yiddish speaker in Mexico and immigration to the United States as a Hispanic Jew.

Also of note is *The One-Handed Pianist and Other Stories* (University of New Mexico Press, 1996), a few of which are appropriate for young readers.

Suárez, Virgil. *Spared Angola: Memories from a Cuban-American Childhood.* Houston, TX: Arte Publico Press, 1997. Impressionistic reminiscence, appropriate for young readers. Novels appealing to older audiences are *Latin Jazz* (Morrow, 1990), *Havana Thursdays* (Arte Publico Press, 1995), and *Going Under* (Arte Publico Press, 1996).

Acknowledgments

Anthologies are collaborative efforts in every sense of the word. First and foremost, I want to thank Marc Aronson, dear friend and highly intelligent editor, for the invitation to put together this volume. His passion for evolving languages and cultures is unmatched, and his endorsement of an endeavor for middle schoolers wherein English and Spanish interact, a topic I've turned into a way of life, is appreciated *de todo corazón*. He was my conscience all along the way, and through a flux of electronic messages and phone calls offered incisive comments on the overall structure as well as specific entries. I'm proud to have produced *Wáchale!* under his imprint at Cricket Books. Thanks too to Jennifer M. Acker and Joëlle Dujardin for the editorial assistance, to Carol Saller for her patience and meticulous eye during the copyediting and production process, to Dominique Kaschak for keying the manuscript effortlessly, and to Héctor García, my admired former student at Amherst College, for the consistency of his look at *el español* and also the Spanglish.

Along with the publisher, I gratefully acknowledge permission to reproduce the material in this volume. Every effort has been made to contact copyright owners. In the event of an omission, please notify the publisher of this volume so that corrections can be made in future editions.

Behar, Ruth, "The Jewish Cemetery in Guanabacoa." First published in *Tikkun Magazine,* July-August 1993. © 1993 by Ruth Behar. Spanish translation by Ruth Behar, in *Poemas que vuelven a Cuba/Poems Returned to Cuba* (Matanzas, Cuba: Ediciones Vigía, 1995). Used by permission of the author.

Candelaria, Nash, "Dear Rosita," from *Uncivil Rights and Other Stories* (Tempe, AZ: Bilingual Press, 1998). First published in Americas Review, vol. 19, no. 2 (1994). © 1998 by Bilingual Press/Editorial Bilingüe. Used by permission of the publisher.

Colón, Jesús, "Kipling and I," from *A Puerto Rican in New York and Other Sketches* (New York: International Publishers, 1982). © 1961 by Masses and Mainstream, © 1982 by International Publishers. Reprinted by permission of the publisher.

Espada, Martín, "Coca-Cola and Coco Frío," from *City of Coughing and Dead Radiators* (New York: W. W. Norton, 1993). © 1993 by Martín Espada. Spanish translation by Maribel Pintado-Espiet. Used by permission of the author.

Gamio, Manuel, "Life, Trial, and Death of Aurelio Pompa," from *Testimonio: A Documentary History of the Mexican American Struggle for Civil Rights,* edited by F. Arturo Rosales (Houston, TX: Arte Publico Press, 2000). © 2000 by Arte Publico Press. Originally included in *The Mexican Immigrant, His Life Story: Autobiographic Documents Collected by Manuel Gamio* (Chicago: University of Chicago Press, 1931). Used by permission.

García-Camarillo, Cecilio, "Talking to the Río Grande," from *Selected Poetry of Cecilio García-Camarillo,* introduction by Enrique R. Lamadrid (Houston, TX: Arte Publico Press, 2000). © 2000 by Arte Publico Press. Used by permission of the publisher.

González, Jovita, "Tío Patricio," from *The Woman Who Lost Her Soul and Other Stories,* edited, with an introduction, by Sergio Reyna (Houston, TX: Arte Publico Press, 2000). © 2000 by Arte Publico Press. Used by permission of the publisher.

Hinojosa-Smith, Rolando, "Sweet Fifteen." © 1988 by Rolando Hinojosa-Smith. First published in *Texas Monthly,* vol. 16, 1988. Used by permission of the author.

Hoffman, Martin, with Woody Guthrie, "Deportee." Translated by Melquíades Sánchez. From *A Plane Wreck at Los Gatos* (Deportee). Words by Woody Guthrie; music by Martin Hoffman. TRO © copyright 1961 (renewed), 1963 (renewed), Ludlow Music, Inc., New York, NY. Used by permission.

Hospital, Carolina, "My Cuban Body." First published in *Latina* magazine. © 2000 by Carolina Hospital. Used by permission of the author.

Levins Morales, Aurora, "Child of the Americas." © by Aurora Levins Morales, translated by Ilan Stavans. Used by permission of the author.

Lubitch Domecq, Alcina, "La Llorona," translated by Ilan Stavans. From *Literary Review* (Fall 1999). © 1999 by Alcina Lubitch

Domecq. English translation © 1999 by Ilan Stavans. Used by permission of the author.

Martí, José, "Simple Verses," from *Versos sencillos/Simple Verses,* translated, with an introduction, by Manuel A. Tellechea (Houston, TX: Arte Publico Press, 1999). Used by permission of the publisher.

Martínez, Demetria, "Fragments," from *Breathing Between the Lines* (Tucson: University of Arizona Press, 1997). © 1997 by Demetria Martínez. Used by permission of the publisher.

Martínez, Dionisio D., "Starfish," from *El Coro: A Chorus of Latino and Latina Poetry,* edited by Martín Espada (Amherst: University of Massachusetts Press, 1997). © 1997 by Dionisio D. Martínez. English rendition by Dionisio D. Martínez. Used by permission of the author.

Mora, Pat, "Corazón del corrido," from *Agua Santa/Holy Water* (Boston: Beacon Press, 1995). © 1995 by Pat Mora. Used by permission of the publisher.

Morales, María Eugenia, "'Twas the Night." © 2001 by María Eugenia Morales. Used by permission of the author.

Obejas, Achy, "Sugarcane." © 1983 by Achy Obejas. Spanish translation by the author and Argelia Fernández. Used by permission of the author.

Ortiz Cofer, Judith, "Kennedy in the Barrio," from *The Year of Our Revolution: New and Selected Stories and Poems* (Houston, TX: Arte Publico Press, 1998). © 1998 by Judith Ortíz-Cofer. Used by permission of the publisher.

Palés Matos, Luis, "Black Dance," from *Selected Poems/Poesía selecta,* translated, with an introduction, by Julio Marzán (Houston, TX: Arte Publico Press, 2000). Used by permission of the publisher.

Pau-Llosa, Ricardo, "Frutas." First published in *Kenyon Review,* vol. 13, no. 3 (1991). Included in *Cuba* (Pittsburgh, PA: Carnegie Mellon University, 1993). © 1991, 1993 by Ricardo Pau-Llosa. Spanish translation by Ricardo Pau-Llosa. Used by permission of the author.

Perdomo, Willie, "Harlem River Kiss." © 2001 by Willie Perdomo. Used by permission of the author.

Ríos, Alberto Alvaro, "The Lemon Story," from *Capirotada: A Nogales Memoir* (Albuquerque: University of New Mexico

Acknowledgments

Press, 1999). © 1999 by Alberto Alvaro Ríos. Used by permission.

Rodríguez, Luis J., "La Vida Loca," from *Always Running: La Vida Loca, Gang Days in L.A.* (Willimantic, CT: Curbstone Press, 1993). © 1993 by Curbstone Press. Used by permission of the publisher.

Sánchez, Rosaura, "jac$in$the$bag," from *He Walked In and Sat Down, and Other Stories,* by Rosaura Sánchez, translated by Beatrice Pita (Albuquerque: University of New Mexico Press, 2000). © 2000 by the University of New Mexico Press. Used by permission of the publisher.

Serros, Michele, "Mi problema," from *Chicana Falsa, and Other Stories of Death, Identity, and Oxnard* (New York: Riverhead Books, 1998). ©1993, 1998 by Michele Serros. Translated by Melquíades Sánchez. Used by permission of the publisher.

Soto, Gary, "Mexicans Begin Jogging," from *New and Selected Poems* (San Francisco: Chronicle Books, 1995). © 1995 by Gary Soto. Translated by Ilan Stavans. Used by permission of the author.

Stavans, Ilan, "Oy! What a Holiday!" from *The Inveterate Dreamer: Essays and Conversations on Jewish Culture* (Lincoln: University of Nebraska Press, 2001). First published in *Sí! Magazine* (1995). © 1995, 2001 by Ilan Stavans. Used by permission of the publisher and the author.

Suárez, Virgil, "Ricochet." © 2001 by Virgil Suárez. Used by permission of the author.